What is Polio?

Polio is a major health problem and a deadly infectious disease
prevalent in several countries. It is a viral illness that can lead to
paralysis, limb deformities, breathing problems or even death. The Polio
virus resides only in humans and passes on to the environment in the
faeces of someone who is infected. Polio is still endemic in three
countries, i.e., Pakistan, Nigeria and Afghanistan and rarely found in the
rest of the world. Pakistan is considered as the exporter of Wild Polio
Virus (WPV) with highest number of Polio outbreaks among endemic
countries. With the start of World Polio Eradication Initiative in 1988,
the number of polio cases has been reduced up to 99% worldwide until
now. In 2015, Pakistan has shown a decrease of 70-75% in number of
polio cases as compared to previous years which is the result of good
governmental initiatives. Militant organizations such as Tehreek-e-
Taliban Pakistan, Al-Qaeda and Boko Haram movement of northern
Nigeria are a major hurdle in the eradication of Polio from these
countries. The misconception of people about the Polio vaccine,
insecurity within the country and poor health system are the reasons for
the failure of Polio eradication campaigns in these regions. Awareness
campaigns about Polio for locals and development of proper health
system will help in the eradication of Polio. Once Polio is eradicated,
about 40-50 billion dollars can be saved globally. With strong
commitment, seriousness and good initiatives, Polio will soon be
eradicated from Pakistan.

In recent years traces of the virus was found in the waste water in
London. Research was carried out and many thousands of children
hadn't received the vaccine. The nightmare was returning.

The generation that came after me don't realise how this dreadful virus
can be. I remember it well. Recently a man died in his eighties in the
U.K. He died from old age. He had Polio early in his life and spent the
rest of his life in an iron lung. He was one of the more serious cases
where he became paralyzed but statistics tell us that 1 in 5 reach this
stage.

Pontllanfraith
Rotary

What is Rotary?

Rotary was founded 23rd February 1905 at Unity Building, Chicago, Illinois, USA by Paul P. Harris. It is a non-political and non-religious organisation open to all. There are around 35,000 member clubs worldwide with a membership of approximately 1.2 million individuals known as Rotarians. (These figures change).

Rotary launched Polio Plus in 1985 and was the founding member of the Global Polio Eradication initiative in 1988. When James L. Bomar jr., then Rotary International president, put the first drops of vaccine into a child's mouth; Rotary's first Health, Hunger and Humanity (3 – H) Grant Project was underway.

The Bill & Melinda Gates Foundation joined with Rotary with a promise that for every dollar Rotary gave to Polio Plus the Gates Foundation would give two dollars. To date over two billion dollars has been raised by Rotary and the Gates Foundation to help with the eradication of this dreadful disease.

....

Acknowledgements:-

Brian Saunders:- a respected Rotarian who understands how Rotary has worked to eliminate Polio in the world. He is also a retired Bank Manager who guided me through parts of this book that involved re-location of Bank Managers. Thank you Brian.

Graham Jones:- A renown player, administrator in Welsh Bowls and currently Patron of Monmouthshire Bowling Association. Graham has also been Welsh Bowling Association President 1991. When I think of a leader I think of Graham. Always a gentleman and when I searched for a bowler for my book, it had to be Graham. A good friend. Thank you Graham for giving your permission to use your name and your achievements in this book.

Jim Merritt:- Jim lives not far from me but I didn't meet him until I joined a writing group locally. When Jim offered to read through my book I was grateful. You never seem to see your own errors when writing. Thank you Jim.

Noel Tippett:- Anyone who knows my husband, Noel Tippett, will agree when I say his first love is bowls. As his wife, he tells me otherwise but I have no problem with his obvious love and dedication to the game. It has made him the man he is and that's fine by me. On this occasion I must bow to his expertise. I could not have written this book in such detail concerning rules and game plans etc. without him.

He tells me it all started when he was a boy; he adored his Dad and wanted to go with him when he went up to the bowling green in Rhymney Park. He learned from an early age that he must be on his best behaviour at the green and judging by what I've been told about him as a boy that wasn't easy for him. His Dad, Haydn, was held in high esteem in the Rhymney Gwent Bowling Club, as was his Dad before him, Robert Tippett.

Noel took me regularly on holiday to Aberystwyth in the summer, and yes you've guessed it, for the annual bowls tournaments. In Plas Crug Bowling Green there is a tree planted in Haydn's honour. I didn't have the pleasure of knowing him but judging by what people say he was a great guy and excellent bowler. The pictures on the wall in the pavilion tell some wonderful stories of days gone by.

I did a little research into the history of bowls and origins of the game. I discovered it had been played by the Egyptians. There was vague evidence that spherical shaped artefacts were found in tombs circa 5,000 B.C. This is clearly conjecture and the purpose of their find is a matter of opinion rather than fact; but interesting none the less.

The game of bowls has been played in the U.K. since the 13th century. Its popularity waxed and waned until the mid 19th century when it started to become popular again, especially in Scotland. The Scots developed flat greens and drew up rules which remain largely unchanged.

The most famous story connected to bowls is that of Sir Frances Drake and the Armada. On the 18th of July 1588 Drake was playing a game of bowls at Plymouth Hoe when he was notified that the Spanish Armada was on the move.

He made a decision to finish the game; which he lost. After the game Drake left Plymouth Hoe and embarked on that famous battle, which he won. A good story - believe what you will.

When I decided to write my fifth book, my dream was to donate all profits to Polio Plus, a charity that saves lives. I needed a market so I had a brainwave. Write about Bowls (a subject I know nothing about but I know a man that does).

My first two novels were 'Orchid of Death' and 'Deadly Relations' both murder mystery stories with a twist. They have sold in the U.K., Europe and U.S.A. I have also written a book of short stories 'Memories and Make Believe' and a book of Poetry.

If you are reading this book, which you have purchased. Thank you for helping the cause and ENJOY!!!

Chapter 1

It All Started in Finchley!

Helen was born and raised in Finchley, north London and met Mike when he moved nearby, with his mum and dad. Mike's dad was a bank manager and moved between branches. Every bank he had managed was known for an exemplary workforce. Mike's dad's name was Barrie and he was a good soul with the patience of a saint. He was a listener and, in some ways, a father figure to the younger staff; a man who nurtured as he taught.

Barrie could be given a branch to manage in Wales then be requested to move to a branch miles away five or so years later. Relocation was often a great upheaval for families but the bank was always sympathetic, especially where children were concerned and, of course, their education. Barrie adored his wife, Alice, and son, Mike. He was always grateful for the support he had from them both regarding the periodic upheavals. Alice always took over the management of every move.

This exact scenario happened to Mike and his parents when they were living, quite happily in Monmouthshire. They had been settled in Wales then after several years were requested to relocate. As it happened, Mike was coming to the end of his high school education so the timing wasn't too bad and London had more to offer the family in many ways. So they made their way to Finchley where Mike found Helen.

After several years of courtship and the completion of his university education, Mike proposed to Helen. Both families were delighted. The couple married and had their two sons, Matthew and Joseph. Helen became a stay-at-home mum and Mike worked for an energy company which paid well. Their life was perfect.

Many years later when the boys were married and settled, they started their own families. At this time Mike rethought his future plans, he wanted a more tranquil lifestyle with a desire to leave the hustle and bustle of city life behind.

His parents had passed away and being an only son Mike inherited their property so he took early retirement and convinced Helen that they should move to the country. Their London home was worth nearly a million pounds and mortgage free which meant that along with the money from his parent's home they could have a beautiful house in the Welsh borders and cash in the bank. They spent a long time looking and eventually found a beautiful cottage in the Wye Valley, a place Mike knew very well. It was in the same county that he had spent his teenage years with his dad managing one of the local banks in a nearby town.

It was a beautiful summer's day when they stood outside the house that was to become their home.

'Oh Mike, its perfect. The garden is just the right size, pretty and manageable. There's more than enough room for the boys and their families to stay over; and so quiet and peaceful. It's heavenly and I love it.'

'Okay, okay.' Mike joked as he put his arms around Helen and gave her a squeeze. 'I get it, you want the house.' His smile told Helen he felt exactly the same.

For once their plan was to live life for themselves and to enjoy every minute of it. They soon moved in, with the help of the boys, and put that plan into action.

The town of Monmouth has a population of approximately 10,500 and is situated where the River Monnow joins the River Wye. Monmouth Castle is perched on a hill above the River Monnow and was the birthplace of Henry V. Due to damage in the English Civil War the old castle site was re-used and built over by The Great Castle House. Of course, it was part of England until 1974 but now belongs to the ceremonial county of Gwent in south east Wales and known as Monmouthshire.

After establishing themselves and becoming part of the community the couple took up a few hobbies. Helen joined the local book club and Mike started playing bowls. He had never played the game before but he felt it was time to step out of his comfort zone and learn new things. Had he known what his future held he may have not moved in that direction.

On the days that Helen watched Mike bowling, mainly sunny afternoons, she decided that it was perhaps something she may like to learn at some time in the future. The club had both a men's team and ladies so it was ideal. Mike made good friends within the bowling fraternity and his involvement made them both feel part of the community.

On alternate Saturday afternoons the green would be a hotbed of competition. A league match would take place and a team would come in from another area and always play to win, often extremely competitive and serious. Tension would soon be forgotten when the players enjoyed a meal in the pavilion together, after the game. Mike's team would also travel to other clubs and the same would happen. He was meeting and enjoying the company of many, some of which became good friends.

The men on the club committee were always pleased to have younger members join them. They seemed to have plenty of energy and with a bit of luck it was hoped that they could take over the work involved in keeping the club going. The older members would then be able take it easy and simply enjoy the game of bowls. Although Mike was in his fifties he was considered one of the younger members.

Young members; in their teens and twenties, were always made welcome but the management of these new players wasn't always easy. The older generation were well versed on how to behave on the green and always looked their best. They were called 'the blazer brigade' and turned out, without exception, in their grey trousers, white shirt and the club tie which was their pride and joy as they marched out onto the green; standing tall and proud.

'The blazer brigade' is men who share the belief that their bowling green was somewhere their children and now grandchildren could watch the game in safety, and hopefully play the sport themselves one day. On rare occasions a younger bowler would slip up and use inappropriate language; they would be reprimanded after the game, quite sternly, and told to behave themselves or else.

'Bowling is a game for gentlemen'.

These words would become emblazoned on the young players' minds. Who so ever dared to step out of line would be spoken to sternly.

Plans sometimes go wrong and tempers can fray when competition fever takes over. On one occasion an older, well established player was heard shouting on the green as he walked onto the next rink.

'Where do you think you are young man? You don't use that language in front of ladies and children.'

The angry man continued loudly.

'My wife and granddaughter are sitting over there and I won't stand for bad language.......Ever!'

He was very upset and marched off the green in disgust.

The young man laughed at him and made a rude gesture behind the back of his elder. It could be said that this young man has a lot to learn but at this moment he is lost in the narrow corridor of youth where you think you know everything but have learned nothing.

The perpetrator was summoned to a meeting before the officials of the club that week and given a verbal warning; but also an explanation of acceptable behaviour on the green. It worked out well and proved to be a beneficial learning curve for the young man who minded his language and behaviour thereafter.

Bad behaviour on the green is unacceptable and the County Rules book is often read out to those who step out of line; it normally works. Of course Mike and Helen were older and of the 'well behaved' generation.

The game of bowls was moderately light exercise but a match could last for hours; a game of endurance. Whilst playing several times each week and practicing other days Mike felt it gave him an energy boost that he'd never known before. A new lease of life, in more ways than one.

Apart from bowls Mike and Helen learned about life in their new village and took part in many other activities, but bowling was Mike's favourite.

With many friends to spend time with and his fast development into the worlds of bowls; Mike had found his place in life. He had never bowled before but within a short time he was part of a team, a natural. Before long it was clear that Mike had a good eye for a winning bowl and was playing in the league. He moved from lead to third, then skip in no time. He had learned from the best and was becoming one.

Mike was making his name in bowls. He was pleasant and got on well with everyone. It was also noticed by the selectors that in individual events he had a very good 'shot selection'. He seemed to have a natural ability to manage his use of weight when aiming his bowl.

After bowling for two years Mike was invited to attend a club coaching course. When he had passed the appropriate courses plus his intermediate coach training, it allowed him to train other club members and also the members of the ladies section.

Helen soon made the decision that if Mike was to spend so much time at the green then it was time for her to learn to play too, and who best to teach her than her husband, the coach.

'I've come to a decision Mike. I want to learn to play bowls and I do believe you are the man for the job.' She smiled discerningly as Mike responded.

'The only problem is, darling; you have to do everything I say and no back-chat. Can you manage that?'

Of course that last comment was ignored.

They loved their new life and wanted to enjoy everything together so Mike was delighted when Helen asked him to coach her. That Sunday morning they set off early to have a trial run, before the bowlers turned up.

'You will love playing bowls, Helen, and I'm sure you'll be great.'

'How good I am will depend on you; coach.' She teased.

They had fun together on the green and Mike was right; under his supervision, Helen was a natural.

After several coaching lessons with Mike, Helen felt ready to introduce herself to the ladies club. Both the men's and ladies clubs played on the same green and on occasion they would play mixed games. They just had the one green so the overall club fixture secretary would ensure no clashes occurred.

The pavilion was unusually large with a well equipped kitchen and a dining room to serve the bowlers and their guests a meal after matches. There was also a lounge bar to sit and enjoy a drink. Very nice changing rooms and other facilities were available. The pavilion is also used by other groups during the winter months, by arrangement, which is quite often.

Both the men's and ladies clubs come under the cover of Welsh Bowls and had rules which had to be obeyed. It was essential to have committees to ensure correctness at all times. Coaching was part of this and Mike stepped up to ensure all new players played the game to the best of their ability and, of course, with Health and Safety in mind. Loving every minute of his new life, Mike created and guided good players which helped to make their club members known and respected at National level.

Helen didn't have the same ambitions as her husband and was happy just to play at club level, making friends and helping with the food preparation after the games. During her years as a stay-at-home mum and baking for the family she had become an excellent cook, so it was natural for her to transfer her skills and produce excellent cakes and pastries for the bowlers after their games. The men especially loved her pastries.

Mostly, the men got on well together but there were occasionally differences of opinion between the membership when it was time for selection for an upcoming match. Selectors sometimes had friends or favourites who were not always the best players and this could result in arguments. These arguments could be nasty but never physical. Although Mike wasn't a selector he often encouraged the weaker players to attend his coaching sessions and do his best to support them.

The committee favoured Mike and knew he would become one of their best players. He was selected for all the team games and won quite a few competitions in pairs, triples and rinks.

Mike was a perfect gentleman, kind, considerate and a good bowler. What could go wrong?

Chapter 2

National Triples Game!

It was finals time at the National Championships in Llandrindod Wells and the sun shone down on the bowlers. Only the best played that week but many supporters, in the form of friends and family, were watching. The three bowling greens were going to be busy at the competition venue and every seat around the green was taken, with many standing and cheering their colleagues and friends on.

The men stood tall and proud in their white trousers and shirts. Their club badges stood out on the breast-pocket of their shirts identifying each man and the club he played for. It would be a proud day for the winners and the probability of the losers drowning their sorrows in the pavilion bar later. The friendships grew every year.

Mike's club was playing a triples final on Wednesday afternoon; Bob, Jim and Mike as skip. They were a good team under Mike's directions and had won the triples as a team many times locally and at higher levels.

The semi-finals had been played on the Wednesday morning. Conditions had been challenging, there had been little or no breeze with the sun exploding in a cloudless sky. Temperatures were in the thirties and relentless but Bob, Jim and Mike had done themselves proud securing an almost unbeatable score early in the game. Their standard of play was remarkable and consistent but taking things for granted was something they were all mindful of. The powerful three took the game.

The men enjoyed a hearty lunch in the bowling pavilion and chatted about strategy for the upcoming game that afternoon. Slightly relishing the mornings win but also considering the reputation of the opposing three they would meet in the final; they, also, were an excellent trio and were never going to be a pushover.

'Bob, if we win the 'toss' for the jack make sure to play a long jack. We could do well as a team with this advantage and it will put pressure on the other side.' Mike was clear on what had to be done.

Bob nodded as he responded.

'I know the lead in the other side and he likes a short jack. They're a good team but we will need to have possession of that jack to play it long.'

Mike added.

'If the opposition's lead places the jack short then I need you both to put bowls behind the jack and, if necessary I can use my last bowl to push the jack towards your waiting bowls.'

The teams carried their bags out of the coolness of the pavilion and into the heat of the afternoon sun. The game began.

The first few ends did not go well, the opposition won the toss for the jack and they played a short jack as predicted which was not Mike's favourite type of game; he liked to play a full length green; a long jack. Because of this the opposition took the first three ends and they had the jack, yet again, for the forth. It was delivered gently which gave them another short jack. Mike could see their tactics were as he thought and rallied his team.

He spoke quietly but firmly to his lead.

'We have to win the jack this end. Bob, as lead, you take your time and aim for the jack in order to take it further up the green. A long jack will give us a better chance.'

Bob nodded, they were seven down after three ends so they had time, but a change of play was needed to get them into a controlling position. The opposing team new Mike would try to take control but so far they had the advantage.

When it was Bob's turn to bowl he did as he was told and took his time, he didn't just want to land his bowl near the jack he had to give his bowl some weight in order to send his bowl and the jack further on. With a bit of luck and a good eye it worked, the bowl was delivered with perfection and the jack was now where Jim and Mike wanted it, they took the advantage back by scoring five in one end and won the jack for the next end which gave them the opportunity to place the jack to suit them. Bob was at his best and did what was expected of him.

'Well done Bob!' Supporters shouted and clapped knowing that this was the turning point.

'Show 'em how to bowl boys. Make sure they have to stretch to a long jack. You can do it'. A comment from an onlooker.

The game was close but Mike's team won by five in the end. There were handshakes from the opposing team on the green and pats on the back by their fellow club members as they walked to the pavilion, where the three men enthusiastically discussed their victory over an ice cold pint.

The national games could be exhausting, often two games a day but a win made it all worthwhile.

Helen, Mike's wife, and Jim's wife, Emily sat together and enjoyed the sun for a while after the game. They knew the conversation between the men would be about the game so they thought it better for them to get it out of their system. At the same time they were very proud of their men. Their game plan and perseverance got them through which won them the game.

The wooden benches were not exactly comfortable for long periods of time so the two ladies had brought their own canvas chairs and were more than happy to sit in the sun a little while longer. The fact that they understood the game of bowls made it more interesting to watch.

'There will be celebrations tonight Helen.'

Emily shook her head and laughed as she spoke.

'Beer and reminiscing, all night long.'

Helen and Emily knew their husbands would carry the excitement on into the evening, laughing and storytelling getting louder as the beer flowed.

Emily was younger than Jim and very attractive. They didn't have children and she worked full time as a beautician in Monmouth. The job required her to look good which she seemed to do with ease.

They lived in a large detached house in the countryside with several acres of land with a successful business which Jim had shared with his late wife, who had suddenly and sadly died of cancer a number of years earlier. When Jim met Emily he had been alone for some time, although he wasn't particularly looking for a wife, meeting Emily changed his life completely and they seemed to be right for each other.

Jim had done well for himself in life; although the house was passed to him from his late parents he continued to run the horse breading business his dad had set up extending it to include riding lessons for all age groups. It had turned out to be popular and very lucrative.

Chapter 3

A Pattern was Forming!

Helen and Emily had become good friends even though there was a considerable age difference. Emily didn't play bowls during the days because of her job, but enjoyed the social activities which included many evenings in the pavilion bar.

On Wednesday afternoons when the ladies league had a home game Emily would join them straight from work. Mike and Jim were always there too, watching the game. When the away side had eaten their fill of the buffet they'd head for home and Helen would quickly replenish the buffet table from her extra supplies in the fridge, for their own supporters to enjoy at leisure. This is a common event and the selling of alcohol also means high takings for the bar.

There is always plenty of competition during a game but mostly a friendly atmosphere off the green. Occasionally a bowler having a bad day would sometimes hold a grudge if he lost a game he needed to win, and on occasions sometimes even rude to an opponent; but that behaviour is rare and discouraged. Of course, in the game of bowls there are winners and losers just like in any other sport.

Bowls is a game for all ages and creates a passion in players. From short friendly 'roll ups' to serious league games and the National competitions. Along with the fun and fellowship of the game there is also hard work needed to keep the players in good condition. Practice is the best way to maintain a good standard and earn respect from others.

Of course, the green itself has to be kept in first class condition and the area around the green needs to always be kept clean for spectators to sit and enjoy the observational experience. The perimeter hedges have to be trimmed and the flower beds well watered in the dryer summer months and then there's the pavilion. The building needs constant maintenance and the public areas must be kept clean and litter free; not to mention stocking the bar.

Most bowlers are dedicated to their game and don't shy away from rainy days, although torrents are mostly avoided. The greens are used only during the spring and summer, however there are often rainy days in Wales in those seasons.

On such days the bowlers would emerge from the pavilion changing rooms in their waterproof jackets and trousers with a cute little waterproof hat, and just get on with the game.

Mike and his parents had lived in the town of Monmouth for over five years in Mike's late teens but he knew very few people from back then, although that didn't stop him reminiscing about the past and his time there. Helen had also found happiness and contentment in Wales and loved showing her family off when they visited. Their dream of spending their retirement in paradise had come true.

If it's possible to measure friendship between couples then Jim and Emily were their best friends. They were so alike in the way they lived their lives; hard working and fun loving. Jim had met Emily for the first time at his daughter Kate's wedding. Kate worked with Emily, who was her bridesmaid. It was a bitter sweet day for Jim because his wife was not by his side and he missed her so much.

Jim and Emily's relationship developed with Kate's blessing. It was meant to be, and their age difference didn't seem to matter. With her long dark hair and perfect figure Emily could have taken her pick of any man but she fell in love with Jim. Their relationship grew out of friendship. Jim had taken things slowly at first, he believed that Emily was more than he deserved and found it difficult to believe her when she eventually said she was in love with him. It wasn't long after that he sealed the deal. They were sitting in his garden enjoying a bottle of Chablis on a summers evening. As Emily sipped the wine, the ring sat at the bottom of her glass.

Her face broke into an enormous smile when she suddenly saw it.

'Is this what I think it is?'

Jim emptied the glass of Chablis over his palm, catching the ring carefully. At the same time slipping down on one knee.

'My darling Emily. Will you make me the happiest man in Monmouthshire by marrying me and making my life complete?'

Emily's smile turned to tears of happiness as she whispered.

'Yes please, but don't you mean 'happiest man in the world'?'

Jim slipped the ring on her finger and although he denies it, he actually had a tear in his eye too.

Just like Jim to be an old romantic but when his friends heard the story they teased the life out of him.

Although Emily always had a smile on her face and enjoyed being with friends, there was a sadness she hid from sight. She had lost her mother, Joan, to cancer a year before she met Jim. Joan had no siblings and her parents had died when Emily was small. Losing all of her family left Emily vulnerable and she clung to her friends. Meeting Jim through his daughter Kate was a Godsend and they shared that common bond of losing a loved one. They both needed love in their life; and now they had it.

Their quiet wedding was organised by Kate and Emily and went smoothly on a mid-September day at the end of the bowls season, of course.

Jim and Emily enjoyed married life and they truly believed that nothing could go wrong now that they had each other, but life is like a jigsaw; never complete until all the pieces are fitted together.

Chapter 4

Suspicions were Aroused!

After the winter break a new season started in the spring with all players eager and ready to win more trophies and enjoy a successful summer. Everything was going to plan and the first game in the weekly league left them triumphant. As the season progressed their high standard continued and so did the celebrations in the pavilion bar.

It was a Wednesday evening, mid season, and the ladies home team had just enjoyed a good win. The wine was flowing in the pavilion and, although just a spectator, Emily had enjoyed a little too much. She had had a hard day in the salon and wanted to forget her worries. Embarrassingly for her, her manner became aberrant and she was unconsciously dropping her guard. It was not like Emily to behave in that manner but things were weighing heavily on her mind.

Helen was also a little worse for wear after a few glasses of red wine, so fortunately she was oblivious to Emily's behaviour. The ladies in the club had noticed that there were 'looks' between Mike and Emily and watched them carefully. The gossip began. There was sometimes a little flirting between the sexes and mostly it was harmless, but some of the ladies were jealous of Emily's good looks and they exaggerated matters a little, causing unnecessary friction and little bad feeling.

That particular evening the ladies were on top form and watched the couple carefully. Their powers of observation were well rehearsed by now. Emily stood up and announced that she was off to the ladies. She walked to the other side of the pavilion where there was a short corridor, then two doors. One with Gents on and the other with Ladies. After a few minutes passed Emily emerged and Mike was waiting for her.

'What do you think you're playing at Em? I saw the ladies chatting and looking at you. I also saw you looking at me so others must have too. I don't want Helen involved until things are clear, people will jump to conclusions before we are ready. I'll meet you Sunday to talk. Jim told me he will be busy with the horse fair in Hereford and Helen is spending the weekend at Matthews. I hate lying to Helen but I told her I have to do some coaching; I'll meet you at the usual place.

Now please take things easy and be patient, it will all fall into place and we can be honest with everyone very soon.'

Emily had tears in her eyes as she looked at Mike.

'I just want all the secrets to be over and we can live our lives honestly. I don't want to hurt Jim and Helen.'

Mike's heart melted.

'I know that, darling. It will be alright soon, I promise, but we must get everything clear first.'

As the saying goes 'the wife is always the last to know', but Helen was content with her husband and trusted Mike implicitly. It's true to say that Mike being unfaithful to her was the last thing on her mind.

Suddenly, there was a moment of doubt. Mike and Emily stood in the corridor as Helen approached to use the ladies toilet, unseen by the couple. She stopped in her tracks as Mike seemingly stoked Emily's face. Helen returned speedily to her seat struggling to process what she had witnessed.

By the time the couple returned to their seats Helen was content in accepting that the apparent emotional contact between Emily and her husband was out of kindness on his part. Em. had drunk a little too much and Mike was looking after her; just like the caring man she knew Mike to be.

Amongst the gossip mongers, however, the banter continued but it was just that, gossip without any evidence of what these women suspected to be true. When one of the ladies asked her husband later that night to watch out for any promiscuous behaviour, he put her straight.

'Don't go spreading rumours that you cannot substantiate. I've never seen any 'hanky panky' going on so you and your lady friends should mind your own business.'

Well said but he knew that wouldn't stop them.

Chapter 5

A Hospital Emergency!

The sound of the siren, heard from inside the ambulance, was louder than could have been imagined, and they had a twenty minute journey ahead of them with a patient who appeared to have a critical injury. It was a busy time of day and the ambulance driver swayed from lane to lane, avoiding the cars that were trying, as best they could under the circumstances, to move out of path of the speeding ambulance. The young medic in the ambulance caring for Mike could see that his patient was drifting in and out of consciousness and did his best to keep him focused until they got to the hospital. Time was of the essence.

'Stay with me Sir. Just a few miles to go and we'll be at the hospital. The doctor is waiting and he'll have you well in no time. Can you see me Sir?'

Mike nodded. The young medic smiled at Mike and touched his shoulder gently. Mike closed his eyes and slipped once more into unconsciousness.

It seemed the swelling to Mike's right temple was growing before this young man's eyes; he was fully trained but quite new in practice, to this kind of experience. He wanted to do his very best for Mike and keep him conscious until the A & E doctor had him in his care.

When the sirens stopped the medic was relieved, as this meant they had arrived at the hospital. Looking out of the window he could see a team on their way to assist.

They wheeled Mike into the hospital and speedily down through the corridor to the waiting doctor and his team. The hospital had advance notice of Mike and his injury so everything was in readiness to act quickly.

They took him straight to the X-ray department where a scan showed a small bleed around the temple which was by now quite swollen and slightly bruised. The temporal artery was badly inflamed so they decided that the pressure needed to be relieved. It was a reasonably small procedure but if left untreated could cause serious problems, including blindness or stroke. Mike was conscious at that moment and able to understand the urgency. The operating theatre was the next stop.

By the time Mike returned from surgery, Helen was informed and had been waiting for quite a while; she was more than a little distressed. Sitting at his bedside she held his hand and waited for him to wake up. The doctor came to the room to explain what had been done and the prognosis.

'Hello! Mrs Saunders. I'm Mr Randawa, your husband's surgeon. I wanted to speak with you in person to explain what we've done. I don't know if you've been told what happened to Mr Saunders but it seems he was punched in the head. The trauma caused his temporal artery to bleed. It has now been repaired and should be okay, however, we would like him to remain with us for a day or two just to make sure. Also, because the injury was caused by the action of another person the police have been informed and they may like to speak with you.'

Helen was in shock.

'I don't understand why anyone would hurt my husband, I'm sure it must be a mistake. He was playing bowls at his club's green. It's a gentleman's game and this type of thing just doesn't happen. It has to be a misunderstanding.'

Poor Helen was getting upset, with all that has gone on in the last few hours; it is beyond belief that another bowler would hurt Mike. Everyone loved him, he was the nicest man.

The surgeon continued.

'Will you be staying with your husband, I can arrange for a more comfortable chair for you?'

'I will be staying, but please don't go to any trouble. You've looked after my husband so well and that's all I care about. I can't thank you enough.'

'You're more than welcome Mrs Saunders. Don't be surprised if your husband sleeps through the night, he's heavily sedated.'

Mr Randawa put his hand on Helen's shoulder before leaving her alone with her sleeping husband.

Within the hour a luxury reclining chair arrived as the surgeon promised; Helen was grateful. There was no way she could leave Mike and she had already decided to stay the night. As she sat comfortably at the bedside of her husband deep in her own thoughts, she heard the door opened. It was her two sons who she'd rung earlier to tell them about their dad.

The boys were living with their own families in London. Matt was a journalist and Joe was in finance, both married and in their thirties with each having a wife and two children.

'I didn't expect you to come all this way, boys, but I am grateful.' Helen broke down and hugged her sons.

Matt was the eldest and always took the lead as spokesman for himself and his brother.

'I know, mum, we couldn't leave you alone.'

Helen explained that the surgeon had repaired an artery in their dad's temple and he would be fine, but for a while he needed to be kept under observation. Missing out the fact that it was, apparently, due to a punch, she wasn't even sure herself why she didn't tell them what clearly was a very important fact. Perhaps it was because she needed to know who and why first; if at all true.

The boys stayed until midnight. They could see their mum was getting sleepy and decided they would go back home to London and ring first thing in the morning.

'If anything happens overnight, just ring us mum; we can come straight back.' Joe hugged his mum.

Helen nodded with tears in her eyes.

'Love you mum.' The boys said in unison as they closed the door behind them.

Helen was indeed exhausted but sleep was hard to find. Before relaxing in her chair she sat on the edge of Mike's bed willing him to open his eyes, of course he didn't; so she stroked his hand gently and told him she loved him.

In the chair she found the lever to recline it to a more comfortable position, and tried to relax. Instead of sleep her mind wandered to nicer things. The happy memories of when the boys were born and their early years. The caravan holidays by the sea, in no time they had grown into wonderful young men and Helen reminisced about both their weddings to beautiful young ladies. Then the grandchildren; how both she and Mike adored them. She closed her eyes with a good feeling that everything would be fine, and drifted off with a smile on her face.

Morning came soon and so did the tea trolley. The noise of the squeaky wheels grew louder as it was being pushed down the corridor towards Mike's room. Helen woke suddenly from her night's sleep on the not-so-comfortable reclining chair. As she rubbed the sleep from her eyes Mike started stirring. Running a hand through his hair she whispered.

'How are you feeling, love? Do you remember what happened at the bowls club yesterday?'

'I think I must have fallen and hit my head.'

'Oh no! You were punched. Your vein was damaged and you've had a small operation. No! Not the vein, it was an artery.' Helen corrected herself quickly. 'Do you remember anything? Why you were punched?'

'No! Helen, I do not remember a thing and I need to rest, why don't you go home? I'm fine.' He was unusually stern.

Helen was a little upset at being dismissed so flippantly but left anyway; Mike was clearly okay. She decided to go home for a few hours and ring the boys to tell them that their dad was awake and fine. As she left the building a police car drove up and parked right outside the main entrance.

'Hi!' said Helen as the driver got out of the vehicle. 'Are you here to see my husband?'

'Who is your husband, madam?' Was the curt response.

'Oh! Mr Saunders, Mike Saunders.'

'Yes we are, how is he this morning?'

'Fine, I think. A bit confused though. Do you want me to come back to the ward with you?'

Helen continued.

'The surgeon that operated on my husband is under the impression my husband was attacked. Ludicrous!'

'No, madam. I'm sure we'll find him. Thank you.'

The officer didn't comment on the second part of her statement.

Another officer joined the driver and they walked into the hospital leaving Helen standing there wondering what would happen next.

Until he saw the officers entering his room Mike hadn't realised the incident would be investigated. He put two and two together and realised the hospital was under obligation to report a suspected assault. He had to think quickly. There could be trouble.

He remembered everything that had happened, deliberately keeping the facts from Helen, but telling the officers the truth would get him into more trouble with his wife. He knew they would want a statement from him and was ready for them when they began to explain everything to him.

'Mr Saunders?'

'Yes,' Mike responded weakly.

'I am PC Thomas and this is PC Edwards. We've been asked to take a statement from you regarding an assault yesterday.'

'There's been no assault officers, I fell and bumped my head on one of the benches in the changing room of the pavilion. Bob Baker called an ambulance when he arrived and found me on the floor.'

'So there was no assault? Are you absolutely sure of that Mr Saunders. The doctor told the station officer, when he rang to report the incident, that this type of injury is caused by a direct blow to the temple.'

'Officer,' Mike spoke slowly to emphasise his words.

'I was not assaulted and the doctor has wasted your time. Why on earth would someone try to hurt me? I have no enemies.'

Mike was a convincing liar.

With a huge weight on his mind and deep concern about the future, Mike closed his eyes and tried to clear the confusion from his mind. He knew he owed it to everyone he cared for to sort this mess out right now and be honest. Should he tell Helen and hope for the best or wait until he knew the truth?

Chapter 6

Mike's Release from Hospital!

The hospital had kept Mike under their care for several days. They were now satisfied that it was safe for him to be released.

Mike seemed to have little concern for his physical well-being. He knew he would have to face the music at the bowls club, and that seemed worse. His mind was full of confusion, not from the bump to his head but how on earth it could all be explained. It was such a mess, if only he'd been honest from the start. Secrets never end well.

Mike had his mobile phone with him at the hospital and rang Helen to tell her the good news about him coming home.

'Hi darling, it's me.' Mike adored his wife and never intended to hurt her with such a secret which was growing out of control.

'Hi Mike, any news on when you can come home?' Was her attempt at a bright response.

'That's why I'm ringing, babe. I can come home early afternoon.'

The last few months of Mike's life had been difficult. From the moment Emily had given him the letter their lives became bitter sweet. His first reaction was that it could not be true. When the realisation of it started to sink in; the confusion turned to curiosity. Could this possibly have an element of truth, the answer was maybe. He read the letter over and over and then decided it could not be ignored and it was his duty, to all concerned, to uncover the truth.

Mike was no fool and he knew that there was gossip. Who could blame them? Although both he and Helen seemed to be the ideal couple and projected an image of stability they were newcomers after all. They had both spent the majority of their lives in London and arrived in Wales with pots of money which bought them one of the nicest houses in the area.

Helen picked Mike up from the hospital and they began their journey home. They sat in silence until Helen spoke.

'Jim rang today to see how you're doing. I didn't realise just how close you were, darling, he's rung every day. A bit over the top, I thought.'

Mike thought for a few seconds trying to formulate a plausible response which would deflect Helen's remark.

'Oh, that's Jim, worrying over nothing. I think he might be feeling a little guilty, leaving me to sort out the mess in the men's changing room alone that day but he had an appointment to get to. Bob had promised to take over from Jim but he was late which left me alone for a while. It's lucky he eventually turned up, I could have been lying on the floor for goodness knows how long if he hadn't.'

Mike laughed to lighten the mood but Helen had a quick retort that stopped the conversation in its tracks.

'Anyway, you'll have plenty of time to catch up. I am going over to the pavilion as soon as we get home; it's my turn to give it a good cleaning. Jim is coming over to sit with you for a couple of hours. We'll eat later.'

Mike was not happy with this arrangement but it seemed he had no choice and just said......

'Of course darling.'

After settling Mike in at home and making a pot of coffee for him and Jim, the door bell rang. Helen took her coat off the hallstand and left with just a weak smile and nod of the head as Jim came in.

Helen loved Mike with all her heart but the gossip going on behind her back was rife and gave reason to speculation; of course she knew what they were all saying about her husband. Even worse was the pity; she could see it in their eyes. Mike was making a fool of her and ruining their future in paradise.

The disparity of the whole situation was worrying; with Mike adamant that he fell over in the pavilion and the hospital doctor being sure that the injury to Mike's temple was the result of an assault. There was so much Helen had to process which lead her to speculate; a dangerous situation that only Mike could put right, and must do, before it's too late.

Helen arrived at the pavilion to find it cold and empty which suited her mood and the confusion swimming around in her mind. Thoughts of Mike's apparent betrayal were foremost in her mind and clouding her common sense. For the most part she did little cleaning and sat trying to work out her future if the worst would come to light. Two hours past quickly and she eventually cleaned the floors and tidied the kitchen; then she sat in the club car park for a while before leaving; again trying to make sense of things. The problem was that there seemed to be no sense, which made her angry but also tearful. Emily's face flashed into her mind and the anger grew. Her so called friend was stealing her husband and she had to do something about it.

Every thought was escalating in her mind and something had to be done; and quickly.

Helen didn't want to go straight home; she was reluctant to see Mike and full of dread at what was to be. She was exhausted physically and mentally but needed to relieve Jim of his duties for which she was grateful. When she arrived at the house there were pleasantries for the best part, but Jim left almost immediately to return home. He needed to work this problem out with Emily and move forward, he felt as if a weight had been lifted from his heart and could look to the future once more; now that he knew the truth. Thanks to Mike and his new found honesty......

Mike had shown Jim the letter that Emily's mother had written before her death. Jim understood the incredibility of Mike's situation. There was something surreal about the fact that Mike had wanted to return to the place he'd spent his teenage years. Was it simply fate?

The Letter

My darling girl, Emily,

Since the day you were born, you have been my world. My mum and dad loved you so much but fate took a turn. One day they were with us, the next they were gone. The day your grandparents died in that dreadful car accident it was just you and me against the world; but we got through it and had a good life. You were just one year old and sadly had no memory of Grandparents who adored you.

The last thing I want to do is hurt you but if you are reading this then I have passed away and there is something important you need to know.

Please remember, I love you very much and kept the secret for so long because I really thought it better you didn't know. Now that you are alone, with no family to comfort you, I believe it's time to tell you the truth.

I let you wrongly assume that your father had been in the car with Nan and Grandpa. You would have been too young to remember your father even if he had lived with us, so I let you believe a lie. I took the easy way out and as the years went by it became more difficult to tell you the truth, until now. He wasn't in the car that day.

You needn't be alone anymore. Of course the choice is all yours whether or not you try to find him.

I met him at school, we were in the same class for certain subjects and we seemed to get on well together. We were young and impetuous, thinking that life was good and nothing could go wrong. I'm not saying we had planned to spend the rest of our lives together; we were nowhere near that stage. We just had fun.

His dad was a bank manager and in those days they seemed to move around the country only settling in one place for five or so years then they would move on.

We spent one Sunday near the river enjoying a picnic that I had put together. It was the best day of my life. We actually just lay in the sun talking for most of the time until it was time to leave. He thanked me for the picnic, kissed my cheek and held me close. It didn't end there; the details are irrelevant but it's safe to say that on that day you were conceived.

We saw each other the next day at school, and of course, I hadn't even considered the fact that I could be pregnant, so no more was said.

After several weeks I realised there was something wrong and tried to build up the courage to speak with him. We went to a local cafe one afternoon after school; he said he had something to tell me, before I could tell him the news.

As we drank our coffee he told me, quite cheerfully, that he and his family were moving on. He had known for a while that a move was imminent, but all was now arranged and they were leaving the following week.

I sat, frozen, with a fixed smile on my face; in complete confusion. I said nothing and I never saw him again after that day. He didn't suggest keeping in touch and I didn't ask him for his new address; all I knew was, he and his parents were going to London, somewhere, because his father had been offered a larger bank to manage. It was the end and I was left pregnant and alone.

I often wondered what he would have done if he had known about you. He was a lovely person but young and starting a new life. I just couldn't bring myself to say the words.

However, I believe now is the time to give him a choice, and the chance for you to know your father.

His name is Michael James Saunders. His father was Barrie and his mother was Alice. They may well have moved several times more but the last place I know for sure was

London. Finchley seems to ring a bell but I can't be sure. All I know is his dad worked for Lloyds bank.

Do with this information what you will, my love. I hope you can find it in your heart to forgive me for keeping this from you for so many years or maybe you can at least understand why. I don't believe Mike and I were truly in love and it would have been wrong to marry without it. We simply made a youthful mistake. I was the lucky one to have seen you grow into a beautiful woman.

Always remember, I have loved you dearly every day of my life and hope you find true love yourself one day.

Your loving Mother X

Chapter 7

Horror Met Jim at the Door!

Driving home from Mike and Helens his heart was, at last free from anxiety.

As he drove up the long driveway he had a great big smile on his face and couldn't wait to hug Em; it was starting to get dark. He stopped at the house and he could see the front door was wide open. Emily felt vulnerable in the large house alone and always kept the doors locked. Jim began to panic as he ran into the house calling Emily's name.

Shouting as he ran he saw that the door to the lounge was open. He hit the light switch and there she was.

'Em!' He screamed. 'Oh my God!' Emily was lying on the floor face up with her head on the stone grate and blood running over the floor from her head.

Jim felt nauseous as he moved seemingly in slow motion to her side. Her eyes were wide open and her body cold. His reaction was futile, but he tried anyway. Opening her mouth he gave her his breath and pumped her chest, not really knowing what to do but feeling the need to do something; anything.

Jim stopped and called her name as he lay over her body and sobbed; wishing he could just close his eyes and be with her on her journey.

It was just minutes but felt like an age as he moved to sit alongside her. He tried to work out what had happened. It must have been a robbery and Emily had been their victim.

He was desperately confused but his evaluation of what had happened encouraged him to ring the police and waste no more time. Anger at whoever did this dreadful thing to his beloved consumed him, along with the agony of his loss.

When the police arrived, the front door was still open and they walked in to find Jim sitting on the floor next to the body of his wife and covered with her blood. It didn't look good.

One of the officers took Jim into the kitchen and sat with him trying to calm his agitation. His speech was incoherent and his hands shook. The officer made him a cup of sweet tea; apparently good for a shock.

The officer spoke first.

'Is there anyone we can call to be with you, Sir?'

Jim tried to think.

'Yes, my daughter. Her number is in the phone under Kate.'

After that was done Jim seemed to relax a little and started to talk.

'I've been at a friend's, he's not well and his wife had to go out so I sat with him. His name is Mike and he's just come out of hospital this afternoon. Helen, his wife, had to clean the bowling pavilion so I stepped in. I drove straight home to find this.'

He began to ramble and became incoherent. His eyes filled with tears.

'If I catch those burglars I'll kill them. You'd better find them first.'

The officer was making a few notes as Jim spoke.

'Sir, we have a forensic team cordoning off the house and it would be less painful to you if there is somewhere you can stay overnight.'

They remained in the kitchen, for what seemed an age, where the officer tried to keep Jim as calm as possible. With that, Kate could be heard talking to a police officer in the lounge, who told her to go into the kitchen where her dad was.

Seeing her father so distraught was upsetting, they hugged and the emotion of the moment was powerful.

'You'll come home with me, dad.'

Jim was concerned about Kate, as Emily was not only her step mother but had also been her work colleague and best friend for many years.

It was a lot for them both to take in but Kate knew her dad needed her help and she was there for him. Although clearly upset she drove to hers and Simon's home in Usk chatting to her dad as they travelled, trying to keep him focused.

Simon heard the car pull up and went out to greet them. He had only a small amount of information regarding what had happened as yet, and didn't push them for details. He hugged them both, waiting until they were settled in the lounge with yet another hot, sweet tea when they began to talk. It was increasingly upsetting for Jim and Kate but very necessary to get the facts straight while they were still fresh in Jim's mind.

Simon had spent all his working life in law. He was currently working as a Prosecution Barrister for the Crown Prosecution Services. He understood the importance of getting the facts recorded before they were forgotten or confused, as often happens with memory recall.

'How could this have happened?' were the only words that came out of Jim's mouth. Kate said nothing.

Simon took the situation in hand.

'Jim, as things are fresh in your mind maybe we should make notes of events leading up to you going home and finding that the house had been broken into.' At this stage he didn't mention Emily.

'I'm not sure it had been broken into, Simon. The door was just open wide as I approached.'

Simon had known Jim for many years as a father-in-law and a friend. He knew exactly what Jim would have to go through in the coming days and weeks and felt he would struggle to cope. It was important that Jim get the details straight in his head in readiness for what was to come; there can be no mistakes. What Jim didn't realise at this time was that if there was no burglar then he would be the prime suspect and would be faced with uncomfortable questioning by well trained police officers whose job it was to dig deep until the truth is uncovered. Personal questions would be asked about Jim and Emily's life.

In the years that Simon had been part of the family he had grown to love and respect Jim. His love for Emily was, to Simon, clearly strong but to a stranger that wouldn't be so obvious. It was Simon's intension to prepare Jim by encouraging him to be precise and confident when questioned by the police. He had to be honest but strong and deflect any suspicion they might have that he is the perpetrator.

Simon noted times and actions for the whole day leading up to the discovery of Emily. They also talked about the reason Helen had asked Jim to sit with Mike. Could someone be managing events which resulted in making Jim's own home more vulnerable? Kate sat close to her dad holding his hand, her hand was trembling.

'Why did you go to Mike's alone rather than take Emily with you?'

Jim put his head in his hands and before he could speak Simon continued.

'Did Helen and Mike get on, did they quarrel?'

Jim responded honestly.

'No, they seemed to be happy together and I've never known them quarrel; but who knows what goes on behind closed doors? I felt they were good friends to us.'

Jim flung his hands in the air in desperation.

'There's something I have to tell you Kate; it's serious.'

It took Jim a while to get the story out into the open for the first time regarding his long felt belief of a liaison between Mike and Emily ending with an admission that he had been wrong. The facts of which had been made clear to him that very afternoon by Mike.

'Most of the bowls club members were gossiping about Mike and Em. and when I found out, I was the one that had punched Mike to the side of his head creating a serious injury. I regretted hitting him, of course, and when Helen asked me to sit with him I intended apologising.'

Jim took a deep breath and continued.

'There's been no affair. Mike showed me a letter that afternoon, to Emily from her mother, Joan. The letter had been in the care of a solicitor with instructions to hand it to Emily on her mum's death. She never mentioned the letter to me. Mike had had a relationship with Emily's mother, Joan when they were in high school together in Monmouth; Emily was the result. When Mike told Joan his family were moving to London with his dad's job she didn't tell him about the pregnancy. There was some disbelief on Mike's part as they had just one sexual liaison, so he asked Emily to go through the procedures of DNA testing. Mike decided that they should wait for the result before telling everyone.'

Simon nodded as Jim spoke and responded.

'So Helen didn't know anything about Emily possibly being Mike's daughter?'

'That's right.' Jim nodded his head in agreement.

Simon continued.

'Then if she had any inclination of the gossip she could be of the belief that her husband was having an affair with Emily.'

Jim stared wide-eyed at Simon's conclusion, at the same time considering its value. He responded.

'Well! Yes, I suppose so but I would think Helen would confront Mike not what you seem to be suggesting.'

Simon shook his head.

'Her involvement in this dreadful situation must be considered and if she was alone at the bowls club, supposedly giving it a 'super-clean', even though her husband had just come out of hospital, there is no alibi to remove her from being a possible suspect.

'I hate to put this into words, Jim, but the police will consider you to be a person of interest too. A crime of passion.'

Jim's face was ashen at the thought anyone could think that he was capable of such a thing.

'But I was with Mike at the time and there's evidence of a robbery too!'

'No there's not Jim. It's only what you assumed to be the reason for this dreadful mess. In my opinion the murderer was known to Emily and she let that person into the house. Also, by what you have said about the way you found Em. it looks to me to be a dreadful accident. I believe there was a scuffle and Em. was pushed, falling onto the stone grate backwards.'

Kate had sat quietly listening until that moment.

'I don't believe any of that, Simon. No-one who knew Emily well would hurt her, not even accidently. It must be a stranger. She probably opened the door without checking who was there.'

Simon put his arm around Kate's shoulder and pulled her close to console her as he spoke his response.

'I'm playing devil's advocate, darling. Your dad must be prepared when the police ask him to make a statement. He must also be prepared for the upsetting questions they will inevitably ask. We, of course, know he wouldn't hurt Emily but from the police point of view he will be the prime suspect and we need to make them think again. One more thing Jim; was the DNA result positive?'

'Yes, it was.'

After Jim and Kate went to bed that night Simon continued making notes and speculating as to whom in the eyes of the law is the most likely to want Emily out of the picture. Two candidates were obvious. Firstly, Helen is clearly the most obvious, then Jim for a different reason. There could have been an argument with Jim being the aggressor, with no intent to actually maim or kill, which got out of hand by pushing and shoving. The way Jim had described to Simon the position that he had found Emily would mean she was face to face with her attacker.

Emily's body was cold which indicates she had been lying on the grate for a while so if Jim was the guilty one, he must have done it before leaving for Mike's house.

Knowing Jim so well, Simon was guilty of unconscious bias in favour of Jim being the innocent party, but he fought against it by concentrating on the facts. With doubts in mind, on balance he honestly believed the guilty party was Helen, but proving it was another matter.

On the other hand if forensic evidence was found it could have been an attempted robbery; whereby Emily caught them in the act and suffered the consequences. Clearly every option has to be considered and the process could take a long time. The police forensic team are turning the house over looking for evidence of a possible intruder and Jim was on edge awaiting the results.

He couldn't give up.

Chapter 8

The worst was yet to come!

Kate spent the whole night tossing and turning; this was her worst nightmare. Her mind was racing out of control and her heart pounding. There was nothing she could do. If only Mike and Helen had stayed in London none of this would be happening. Her best friend would still be alive and her dad wouldn't have to face being a widower for the second time. Or more to the point why didn't Emily tell her that she thought Mike was her dad, she was, after all, her best friend. Why all the secrecy? All this could have been avoided.

Daylight shone through the window early and it seemed that no-one had slept. Jim, Kate and Simon were gathered around the kitchen table drinking coffee when the phone rang. Simon took the call and listened, speaking only after a few minutes saying.....

'I will, officer. We'll be there.'

The call was expected by Simon but now he had to tell Jim.

'As expected, they want you down the station to answer some questions and make a statement. I've told them that I will attend with you today but I have someone in mind if this business is taken further. My friend and colleague Martin is one of the best defence Barristers that I know and I'm sure he'll take on the job.'

Jim looked exhausted as he spoke.

'Do you think they'll charge me, Si?'

'I don't know Jim, I really don't know.'

They were due at the station at ten o'clock, so they spent a few hours drinking coffee and talking about the notes that Simon had written down during the night; twenty pages or so.

As Simon drove to the police station in Monmouth, the County town, he kept the conversation going; mainly to keep Jim focussed.

'Just be honest about everything Jim, don't leave anything out for them to find later and accuse you of concealing evidence. There won't be any trick questions, as you may expect, but think for a second before you answer anything to ensure clarity and accuracy. If it becomes too much for you, give me the nod and I'll ask for a break.'

At the police station Jim felt his anxiety rising, he was terrified. He could see how things were looking for him when he told the interviewing Detective Sergeant that there were rumours at the bowling green about his wife having an affair with his friend Mike. Jim also realised as he spoke that timescale came into the equation. He knew by the questions the officer was asking that he was calculating that Jim could have murdered his wife before leaving his house to sit with Mike.

It was becoming evident that only when he was at Mike's and he was shown the letter from Joan to her daughter that the secrecy between Mike and Emily wasn't because they were having an affair.

Jim also confessed that he was the one that punched Mike to the head, although Mike had denied it to the officers that had interviewed him in the hospital. Jim was feeling worse by the second and struggled not to get emotional.

The interviewing officer continued.

'If your wife thought Mr Saunders was her father, why didn't she tell you?'

'I can't answer that, officer, but I believe Mike wanted to keep it a secret until they had confirmation with DNA evidence. I suppose he thought there might be a mistake, who knows? Now that I know the truth I feel so bad that I lost my temper and hit out at him, it's really not like me to do a thing like that. Please believe me; I could never hurt anyone enough to cause death.'

There was a silence. Jim held his head in his hand as the police officer gave him a minute to recover.

'How well do you really know Helen Saunders? Is it possible that she knew about her husband's liaisons with Emily? Maybe you were callously used to care for her husband, and she went to your home to confront Emily and not the pavilion as she claims?'

The officer was using various scenarios of what could have happened that day and suggestions that Helen had reason and opportunity to have killed his wife. The D.S. was relentless in his desire to break Jim and get to the truth. He asked Jim questions over and over, even asking him outright.

'Did you kill your wife, Jim? Let's be honest; you had cause.'

'Please, this is too much. All I know is I wouldn't hurt my wife and I truly believe that Helen had nothing to do with my wife's death. You don't know Helen as I do. She is a truly kind person and has been a good friend to Emily.'

'Well sir!' the officer continued. 'There is no evidence to suggest a robbery and everything points to someone, who your wife knew, was let into your home and there was some sort of confrontation that ended with your wife being pushed over and landing on the stone grate in your living room. If it was you then the argument would have taken place before you went to sit with your friend and you believed this would give you an alibi. Is this what happened, sir? Did you have murderous intent?

Before the distressed Jim could respond Simon intervened.

'Officer, unless you are going to execute a charge against my client, we will be leaving. You have been given an honest account of everything that happened that day.'

The two got up and left the police station; knowing the worst was yet to come.

The interview took nearly six hours with two breaks, an experience that would shake the strongest man. The repetition of questions asked in different forms with the intention of breaking Jim and getting a confession was relentless. However with Simon at his side, he got through it. The one thing that worried Jim was the fact that he had shown aggression by hitting Mike, which was considered serious due to his hospitalisation. Would the police think that this was the real Jim, an aggressive bully?

It was clear to Simon that with Jim being the first to attend the police station they were in the process of collecting relevant evidence with no positive information so far, that could convict. They just had theories. The D.S. was feeling his way by asking questions and setting scenarios to see Jim's reaction. A typical ploy, but, in the interest of getting to the truth, very necessary.

The two men were both tired and just wanted to get home and relax; that wasn't to be.

When they arrived home Kate had news.

'I've had a phone call to say Emily's body has left the morgue and is now at the funeral home and ready to be formally identified. How did it go at the station?'

'Not too bad, love.' Simon chipped in before Jim had a chance. 'They got a bit pushy but mainly they just wanted your dad's side of everything.'

Jim smiled at Kate as he spoke but the look on Simon's face told Kate there was more to come.

Kate didn't feel ready to see Emily so Simon stepped up and took Jim to the funeral home.

It was expected that it would be an emotional experience for Jim and Simon was a tower of strength. Emily's body was in a special room used for family viewing. As they were lead into the room a young man told them to take their time, he then left closing the door behind him.

Emily looked beautiful and serene, nothing to indicate that she couldn't open her beautiful blue eyes and smile at the onlookers. It was dreamlike and the only thing that made it real were the tears rolling down Jim's face. His legs couldn't support him and he sat on a chair next to Emily. He touched her hand feeling only distance.

He cried as he spoke.

'I can't believe you're gone, taken from me, my darling. I teased you often that I married you to look after me in my old age, and you'd laugh. I don't know how I can go on without you............

You are my everything. Sleep tight my precious girl, you are safe now.'

Simon touched Jim's shoulder gently as he turned to get up; they both had tears in their eyes. It was a powerful moment for them both.

'It's time to go Simon and help the police to find the person who did this to our Em.'

Simon was emotional at the funeral home and as they drove home in silence he hated himself for the thoughts and doubts creeping into his head. The way Jim re-acted to seeing Emily lying there silently was heart breaking and what you would expect from a grieving husband but his final words didn't fit. Why was she safe now and from whom or what?

Simon's legal training was to examine the evidence from all perspectives. His experience guided him to think that a man who believed his wife was, maybe, having an affair with his friend would be angry with them both; it would seem like the worst betrayal. Kate had seen the crime scene and had told Simon that it appeared Emily had been pushed backwards towards the grate; something that could happen on the spur of the moment with no criminal intent. Simon processed the information and concluded that it was possible that it had happened before Jim went to sit with Mike. Then Mike showed him the letter which changed everything.

Simon felt bad for thinking of things that way but blamed his prosecutor style evaluations and reasoning that he relied on when proving guilt in the courtroom. In reality he asked himself, how could this man he had known and loved for so many years do something like this? A man that had lived in the area all of his life and was known for his honesty and caring. Simon prayed that Jim was an innocent man.

If it wasn't a burglary or Jim then who killed Emily?

Chapter 9

Honesty is the best Policy!

It was 8 a.m. Mike and Helen had sat at the breakfast table for half an hour, in silence.

'Helen.' Mike broke the silenced with well rehearsed words.

'I have something to confess that may cause you to doubt me; but I have always been faithful to you and I truly love you with all my heart.'

He ran his fingers through his hair as he began his story. He owed Helen an explanation and the words had to come out right.

'When I met you in Finchley I was nineteen years old and ready to continue my education in university. We enjoyed each other's company when I was home on visits from Uni. which I always looked forward to. I was falling in love so deeply I sometimes felt scared. The sight of you made me realise you were the one I wanted to spend my whole life with. We were perfect for each other and both our families agreed.

'I didn't have many girlfriends before you and I'd never been in love. When I realised that dad was going to be transferred from Wales I was happy, I didn't feel I personally had anything to stay for. At that time I had been going out with a girl called Joan; nothing serious, mostly we'd just go for a walk or a coffee. When I told her we were leaving Monmouth she didn't seem to mind. Now, I know differently.'

'What are you going on about? I don't care if you had girlfriends before me, that's all in the past.' Helen was getting irritated.

'Please, hear me out. I'm coming to the important part where everything will fall into place.'

Mike continued.

'On one sunny day Joan made a picnic and we spent the afternoon on the river bank, we were intimate, it was the only time. Mum, Dad and I then moved to Finchley and there was no contact between Joan and me. The years went by and when the boys were settled with families of their own we decided to move to the country; we moved to Monmouthshire. We both loved the countryside and made a new life for ourselves. Then we joined the bowls club and made friends. I became good friends with Jim but it took me a while to realise that there was something about Emily that I couldn't quite put my finger on. She had a look of familiarity.'

'You were attracted to her you mean.'

'No darling! Not in the least. But a while after that first meeting with her she started to ask me questions about my past. It was strange. Then she could see that I was getting suspicious and dropped the bombshell. She told me that she believed I was her father.'

Mike waited a minute or two for Helen to think about what he'd said. It was a lot for her to take in. He continued.

'Emily told me her mother's name was Joan. When Joan was told she had terminal cancer and didn't have long to live she wrote a letter. This letter had been placed with her solicitor with instructions to give it to Emily after her demise.'

Mike handed the letter to Helen. Her hand shook as she read it.

'Why didn't you tell me, Mike?'

Mike had tears in his eyes as he spoke the words.

'Because I had to be sure she was right. I arranged for us both to privately see a doctor who could verify with DNA, that I was Emily's father; or not.'

'And are you, Mike?'

'The results were positive but arrived too late, Emily was dead.'

'Oh my God!' Helen reached out for Mike's hand across the table. Was it relief that her husband had not been unfaithful to her that Helen found herself sobbing? They stood and embraced; taking comfort in each other's arms.

Within seconds there was a loud knocking at the front door. Mike opened the door to find two police officers standing there with a police car at the end of the drive.

'We'd like to speak with Mrs Helen Saunders please, Sir.'

Mike's heart skipped a beat as he realised that Helen could be a suspect in the death of Emily. When he turned to call Helen she was right behind him with an ashen face.

'Ah, hello Mrs Saunders. Would you come with us to the station, please? If you feel you need legal support we would advise you to either use the duty solicitor or, of course, your own.'

Helen turned to see Mike with tears in his eyes as she got into the police car. Whatever was ahead for the couple they had each other but would it be enough?

Chapter 10

At the Station!

When they arrived at the police station Mike was seconds behind in his car. They had never had the need for a criminal lawyer before and didn't know one, so the Duty Solicitor was called on. Helen and Mr Bolter, the Duty Solicitor, were allowed some time to discuss the matter before her interview by the Detective Inspector in charge of the case.

'Don't worry Mrs Saunders this interview is procedure and nothing for you to be frightened of. It is the legal obligation of the police to gather all evidence from people who could be suspects or witnesses and establish relevant information to form a picture of what happened on the day in question. I have read the facts of the case and it seems you didn't have an alibi for the time in question. Also, it could be deemed that you have reason to be concerned about the relationship between your husband and the deceased; albeit later to be proven that your husband was indeed the father of the deceased. Is what I've said correct Mrs Saunders?'

Mr Bolter clearly understands the importance of this interview as regards the possible outcome and is aware of the reasons and objectives of the case, but he needs his client to understand too.

'Yes, Mr Bolter you are correct but I never doubted my husband's loyalty to me. His reason for keeping the secret of him possibly being Emily's father, is because he had doubts and was awaiting DNA results. He didn't want to worry me.'

'Yes I understand that but for today this meeting is for fact-finding only. Are you ready?'

'I'm ready.'

Mike remained in the waiting room.

Four hours and one break later Mike and Helen were on their way home. They travelled in silence but Helen gave vent to her feeling when they arrived.

'If you had told me the truth from the beginning I wouldn't have to go through all this. People will think I killed Emily. That's what people do, jump to conclusion without having all the facts. This is more than I can deal with. I know I didn't do it. Do you Mike?'

'Of course I know you didn't do it, you wouldn't hurt a fly.'

Helen jumped in.

'Our new life is ruined. The friends we have made in Monmouth don't really know me. They will think I did it.'

There was little further conversation between Mike and Helen that day. Mike rang the boys after dinner and had a difficult conversation with each of them. Both Matt and Joe were eager to come to Wales and help in any way they could; but Mike reassured them by saying he will ring every night to update them. Mike presented a confident front and the boys seemed to accept their parents could cope alone.

Helen sat in the kitchen drinking coffee and Mike sat in the conservatory alone. In his heart he knew Helen would never hurt anyone deliberately but the facts were that Emily's death was caused by a push that went horribly wrong. In other words an accident; but in law it would be classified as manslaughter.

The following afternoon Mike felt the need to get out of the house for a while. The bowls season was coming to an end and for the past few weeks Jim and Mike had been absent. After an awkward chat with Jim over the phone Mike went to the green to speak with the committee; Jim couldn't face his friends at that time so he didn't go with Mike. There was a game on, just a friendly, so Mike watched until the end sitting on a bench near the pavilion. The rinks finished one by one and the lads walked past Mike into the pavilion.

Mike wasn't sure what to expect. As it happened – a bit of both. Some were dismissive with just a nod of the head as they passed. Others asked how he was; for this he was grateful.

When the visitors left the pavilion, members of the committee remained; it was clear that Mike wanted to speak with them. They sat around a table and he explained in full what had happened, including the police interviews. Mike was clearly distressed.

'I believe I handled the situation wrongly. When Emily told me what she believed to be the truth, that I was her birth father. I asked her not to tell anyone until we had positive DNA confirmation. Meeting in what we thought was secret lead the way to people assuming we were having an affair. At that point we should have told both Helen and Jim what the conspiracy-like behaviour was all about. But we didn't.

I had known Joan, Emily's mum, when I was living in Monmouth with my parents. I was in my late teens and we had a single intimate liaison which ending in pregnancy. I moved to London oblivious of the fact I had left a pregnant Joan behind.

The police have questioned Jim about his whereabouts on the day Emily died. Helen had asked him if he could sit with me for a few hours while she cleaned the pavilion. I had come home from hospital that day and she didn't want to leave me alone. So Jim explained all this to the D.S. Of course he had spent hours with Emily before leaving for my house; but I honestly cannot believe Jim could or would hurt Emily, he adored her.'

Mike shook his head in disbelief as the men looked on.

'The next one to be questioned was my wife Helen. Although she said she was cleaning the pavilion; there's no proof. From the police's point of view she could have been in the building for a while giving the floors a quick wash and then drove to Emily's. I know Helen couldn't hurt Emily but it's the facts that matter. It's looking bad for both of them at the moment.'

The committee members sat in silence. As Mike spoke there seemed to be a look of compassion coming through.

The chairman of the club, Mr Graham Jones, spoke first.

'I'm sorry for the pain you must be in, Mike. You may have handled the matter in the wrong way but your intensions were fair. You have a long road ahead and the outcome may not be good. Either way one family will lose. I'd like to thank you, on behalf of the committee, for your full and frank explanation of events. I can assure you we will curb all gossip within the club and will welcome you whenever you attend. I hope you understand that the duties you carry out as a member will be put on hold until the legal side of this matter is resolved; also, you need to concentrate on the days ahead.'

The meeting concluded and Mike left the pavilion. He walked to the car with tears rolling down his cheeks.

Chapter 11

Jim Pays a Visit!

On the way home from the pavilion Mike stopped at the garage to pick up some flowers for Helen. She smiled when she saw him walking in. It lightened her mood.

'It's a small gesture for all the trouble I've caused you Helen. I've spoiled everything; keeping such a secret from you.'

He held her close. Helen felt warm and safe in his arms and, also, a great weight had been lifted knowing her beloved was always true to her. She felt a little guilt that she had faltered in temporarily believing otherwise.

The door bell rang and Mike went to see who it was.

'Oh! Jim. I wasn't expecting to see you.'

'Can I come in Mike, I want to see Helen?'

'I don't want any trouble, Jim; she's still upset after being questioned by the police.'

Jim marched into the lounge where Helen was sitting; she had heard the conversation at the front door and felt that she really couldn't take much more.

'Helen, I will come straight to the point. I know I didn't hurt Em. Was it you? It's got to be one of us; you must see what the police are thinking. Please can we be honest with each other.'

'I swear Jim, it wasn't me. Please believe me.'

'I want to Helen but you can surely see how all this looks.'

Jim almost fell onto the sofa next to Helen and Mike sat on the chair opposite.

'I just don't know what to do. I told the police when I was being interviewed that I didn't think you could do such a thing, Helen; but it's clearly one of us. It has to be. I don't believe for one moment that you wanted to hurt Emily but I can understand if you were upset and the whole thing was a dreadful accident.'

Jim looked across at Mike.'

'If you and Emily had just been honest when you thought there might be a connection, all this would never have happened.'

'I know that Jim and don't you think I feel really bad about all this?'

Helen reached out to hold Jim's hand as she spoke; to console him and calm things down. His pain was clear and words do little to help, but she had to try.

'We're all suffering Jim. You've lost your wife and I've lost a good friend. There must be something we're missing in all this mess. Maybe there's a totally different reason for an argument with someone. The police seem to believe that there was no intent to seriously harm Emily and definitely no suggestion that the intention of the aggressor was to kill her. If she hadn't been so near the fire grate she would have survived the push. Was there anything going on in her life that made her a target?'

Jim put his head in his hands in despair and mumbled his response.

'Emily was an open book, Helen; she had no secrets until all this.'

'I believe that too; but do you ever really know someone? We mustn't fight each other, Jim. There's an answer somewhere out there that will be uncovered.'

Jim nodded as he responded.

'I am so sorry to come to your home, albeit in desperation, to challenge you. I just feel as if I'm losing my mind because I know it wasn't me.'

Helen put her arm around him and they hugged. Tears were flowing but with the tears came a little relief. Mike watched and shed a tear too.

They sat in silence. Their bodies ached with exhaustion and their faces told a story of confusion.

The telephone rang and broke the silence.

Mike picked it up.

'Mike, it's Allan, I was in the committee meeting earlier and I need to speak to you, it's important.'

'Yes, of course.'

Mike left the lounge and walked into the kitchen as the two men spoke on the phone, excusing himself with a wave of his hand to Jim and Helen as he walked.

Allan sounded upset.

'When I left the meeting I went home and checked the dates in my diary. I needed to confirm what I believed to be true. On the day that Emily was killed I was trimming the hedge at the green. I saw Helen come in through the gates and walk into the pavilion. I also saw her leave two and a half hours later; I was still at it. I nearly said something after the committee meeting but I needed to check the date first.'

'But Allan, Helen said there was no-one there all afternoon.'

'She wouldn't have seem me, Mike. I was outside the pavilion cutting the exterior of the hedge; I used the old hedge cutter rather than the hedge trimmer so it made no noise. It took much longer to do by hand but I could cut the overgrown branches closer. I could see Helen as she walked into the pavilion; but a little too far to acknowledge her verbally.'

'O my God! Thank you so much Allan. I am truly grateful. Can I ring the police station?'

'I'll do it Mike; what's the officer's name?'

'D.S. Johns.'

'Thanks again, Allan.'

'You're welcome, Mike. I'm pleased I can help. You must be going through a bad time.'

'You don't know what this means to me. I can't wait to tell Helen.'

Allan hung up and Mike walked back into the lounge, He noticed that the conversation was a little calmer as he walked in.

Helen and Jim both looked at Mike as he came into the room.

'It's over Helen. Allan Spencer was on the phone. He was at the green on the afternoon Emily died; cutting the hedge.'

'But I didn't see anyone.'

'I know, darling. He was on the outside of the hedge but he saw you come in and leave. The timing matched including your drive there and back, the perfect alibi. He is now ringing the D.S. with his story.'

Jim stood up to leave.

'Well, that's it then. Everyone will believe I did it. How, in God's name can I prove I'm innocent? This cannot be happening to me.'

'Don't go driving in that state Jim. I'll make some coffee.'

Mike got up and walk to the lounge door.

'Don't bother. I know what you're thinking.'

He pushed past Mike and left.

The drive home was difficult for Jim. This nightmare was worsening by the minute. The woman he loves is gone forever and it seems now that the whole world will believe he killed her.

Chapter 12

Another surprise!

Simon and Kate had been sleeping over at Jim's house since the forensic team had gathered all the evidence they could. Both had been concerned that her dad might harm himself if he was left alone, he was not coping well. The loss of Emily was bad enough but being a suspect in her demise was unbearable. Kate was a wonderful, caring daughter and Simon had stepped up to the mark when he was needed. His legal experience was invaluable to Jim.

The couple had what would have been good news to share but hadn't told Jim yet. Maybe now was the time. Something good to share as a family.

Jim was drowning in sadness, with seemingly no escape. As he drove back from Mike and Helen's he was trying to work out how to tell his family that he was now the only suspect left in the picture. He drove up the long drive and stopped outside the front door; Simon had heard his car and went to the front door to open it.

They both joined Kate in the lounge and sat in silence for a few seconds. Jim didn't know how to break the news that he was now the only suspect; so he didn't.

'Jim.' Simon began.

'Kate and I have wanted to share some news with you for a while but with all that's happened we held back. She asked me to tell you that she is feeling a little out of sorts if you had noticed anything. Kate doesn't want you to think that she's neglecting you. The reason she feels a little nauseas is because you are going to be a granddad.' He reached over and held Kate's hand.

Jim broke down and struggled to speak.

'I am so pleased for you both. I know how long you've been waiting and I am truly delighted for you. I really am.'

Simon could see how hard Jim was working at being cheerful.

'There seems to be a 'but', Jim. What's wrong?'

'Where do I start? When I was at Mike and Helen's today they had a phone call from Allan Spencer, a friend who plays bowls at our green and does a little work there. He remembered being at the green the day Helen said she was cleaning the pavilion. He was trimming the hedge from outside the green, and couldn't be seen easily but he had seen Helen walk through the main gate and enter the pavilion, staying for two and a half hours. Helen now has an alibi.'

'But wouldn't there be a noise coming from the hedge trimmer?'

Simon questioned.

'No, he used the shears to trim it.'

They sat in silence. Then Kate got up and left the room.

'Where are you going Kate?'

She didn't stop.

'It's okay Jim she gets a little sick, you know, with the baby.'

Jim nodded.

'But I'm making everything worse, aren't I. And now, even Kate will think I killed Emily.'

Simon took a deep breath and as he spoke he was succinct and to the point.

'We must be clear on this Jim. They will no doubt arrest you. I've told you about Martin; he's one of the best Barristers I know. I'll ring him and ask him to come over as soon as he can. I have already told him all I know, apart from the new evidence that Helen is now out of the picture. We have to be clear on the facts before we go to the police station and Martin will guide you thereafter.'

'I don't think I can do this, Simon.'

'You have no choice, Jim. I'll ring Martin now to see when he can come over.'

The conversation was short and sweet. Martin was in the Crown Court and the matter he's dealing with is coming to an end.

'He'll be here within the hour, Jim. Until then we need to go over all my notes again to get things clear in our mind. Then when Martin gets here we will do it all again. The next few weeks will not be easy but we are in this together Jim; you are not alone.'

Kate made the men coffee and they sat around the table with Simon ensuring Jim understood the journey ahead.

Time went by and most of Simon's explanation of what was to come were discussed.

The doorbell rang.

Martin hugged Simon as he walked into the hall. He was well over six foot and looked the part. Of course, he was just out of the courtroom so his dress made him look even more professional.

'Don't worry, my friend, we'll get this matter sorted in no time.' They walked into the room where Kate and Jim were seated at the table.

'I am so sorry to hear about your wife. Simon said she was a lovely person. The whole situation regarding her demise must be so difficult for you.'

Jim just nodded. Then added.

'I didn't do it, Sir.'

'Please call me Martin. I will do all within my power to ensure the Judge understands what a good man you are. Simon has certainly convinced me.' They both smiled.

'Now, I know Simon has written down the salient points that we can start with.'

'So, Simon, what is this new development you mentioned on the phone?'

'Helen Saunders, the other person of interest has now got an alibi. She was at the Bowling Green that afternoon; it was her turn to clean the pavilion. There was no game on and no-one else in the pavilion so she automatically became a person of interest, considering her position in the investigation. But now it has come to light that a member of the bowls club was trimming the hedge and saw her. I believe that the witness is informing the police of this new information as we speak.

'The gentleman who saw Helen at the green is Allan Spencer. I presume the police will have or soon will be speaking with this witness to make a statement. By what Jim has told me the witness is of good character with no recognisable bias.'

Martin thought for a minute then responded.

'Well, that clearly makes things a little more difficult for us; but not impossible. We will explore other avenues and possibilities. The only thing we can do now is to introduce doubt.'

'This is not a fait accompli.'

Chapter 13

The Battle Begins!

Martin, Simon and Jim started work, the police could be knocking at the door at any time; there wasn't a second to waste. Kate was feeling tired so she had gone upstairs to take a nap. It was hard to see her father in such a position with the probability of imprisonment ahead. The thought of her dad taking the blame for something he clearly hadn't done made her run to the bathroom. She felt the need to go down stairs and simply be there for her dad and hold his hand. But she was so afraid.

Downstairs the men had covered all the details of events on that dreadful day and were almost ready for the knock at the door. It wasn't Martin's job to work out who could have killed Emily; just cast doubt over Jim's presumed guilt and whatever the prosecution would throw at them. Simon knew only too well how the prosecution would present their case; he had prosecuted many similar cases himself, and won. But, of course, there was another option for Jim.

Martin was content that all relevant matters had been discussed, apart from one.

'There is one further option to consider, Jim.' He needed to put this option forward for Jim to consider seriously.

'If you plead 'not guilty' and the jury, having heard the pros and cons of the case find you guilty, then the sentence will be definitely prison and possibly for a long time.'

Jim was visibly upset and responded.

'So I'll definitely go to prison then?'

'If the jury find you guilty, then yes. But there is an alternative.'

'How can there be an alternative, I am not guilty and I should walk free, an innocent man, Martin.'

Martin thought for a moment before coming back with the alternative.

'You can plead guilty with diminished responsibility. I know what you're thinking Jim, but you must appreciate what the jury may be considering having heard the facts. As you probably know, if you plead guilty at your first court hearing then your punishment will be reduced by one third; this could even mean reducing the punishment from imprisonment to a suspended prison sentence, which means you can come home. There is also another consideration as regards a guilty plea. The legal argument for this is as follows:-

'A conviction for manslaughter by reason of diminished responsibility necessarily means that the offender's ability to understand the nature of conduct, form a rational judgment and /or exercise self-control was substantially impaired.'

'I know it's complicated, Jim, but it is worth listening. If a person commits "involuntary manslaughter" then it mitigates the offence and therefore the punishment too.

'The law is clear Jim, and I quote. "The harm caused by any offence that results in a death is immeasurable. The sentence is not a measure of the value put on the life of the victim" meaning simply that even if you commit a crime you can walk away if good reasons are substantiated.

'The choice is yours Jim; Innocent or guilty.'

Jim responded firmly.

'So are you suggesting that even though I did not kill my wife, I should say I did kill her?'

'No Jim, I am certainly not saying that but it is my duty to clarify your choices and the probable results of making them. The choices are up to you entirely, now that I've explained everything.'

Without hesitation Jim responded.

'I will never lie to the world and say I killed my wife when I most certainly didn't. That is my answer Martin.'

'Good decision Jim and one I never doubted you'd make.'

The two men shook hands. There was going to be a battle ahead so the next move was to have a cup of tea.

As they chatted over their tea the doorbell rang.

The officers were invited into the lounge by Simon. They remained standing when the arrest was carried out and Jim was taken to the station with Martin following behind in his black Porsche.

The formality of the meeting was strained and carried out by two senior officers. Recording the clarification of previously discussed matters was important and Jim felt lost and bewildered.

How could this be happening to him?

Chapter 14

Life Goes on!

The chairman of the bowling club called an emergency meeting when he was informed of the development concerning Emily's demise.

Graham, the chairman, had worked for the Welsh Bowls Association at the highest level and is a life member. In more recent years his health prevented him to travel far and wide to attend meetings throughout Wales. He now concentrates on the club he loves and the administration thereof. Of course, he's always ready with good advice when there's an issue, and his knowledge and experience is relied upon.

As the committee gathered in the pavilion, Graham heard the comments of the men in attendance. He brought the meeting to order quickly so that the facts of the events would be discussed and nothing more.

'Gentlemen', Graham spoke loudly and clearly, he had 'walked the boards' in many dramatic performances and knew well how to project his voice, but in a polite manner.

'Please take your seats. The meeting is about to commence and I would appreciate your full attention.'

Graham always received the respect he deserved from his fellow bowlers. They all sat in silence and he began.

'As you all know Mike Saunders, one of our newest members, has been through a traumatic time. But I am pleased to say his wife, Helen, has been cleared of any involvement concerning Emily's demise.'

Graham looked around at his audience and could see their relief.

He continued.

'I have knowledge of a new development regarding the death of Jim's wife Emily. As you all know, Jim found his wife when he returned home after sitting with Mike on his release from hospital. The front door was ajar when he got home which raised immediate concerns for him. Jim entered and found Emily lying on her back with her head on the stone grate in the living room.'

Graham, again, allowed his listeners time to absorb this information.

'Emily sadly died that day. Jim called the police and forensic evidence was clear; there was no trace of anyone apart from the direct family members being in the property recently. There had been no intruder. We discussed the incident briefly at an emergency meeting I had called. The object of that meeting was to avoid speculation by keeping everyone informed of the facts as we know them. At that meeting was Allan Spencer who recalled he was in attendance at the green on that day; cutting the hedges. He said nothing at that time but when he went home he checked the details of his movements with his diary which confirmed that he had seen Helen on that particular day. He then went to the police station with his diary and gave Helen an alibi.'

'We have all known Jim for many years and are saddened that our dear friend is now the only suspect of what comes down to the criminal offence of manslaughter. At a personal level I have to say I do not believe Jim is capable of harming Emily. However the police investigation is looking at Jim as the prime suspect.'

Again Graham took a breath.

'I would ask you all to remain positive and to remember that Jim is and has been a treasured member of this club for many years and a good man. In other words, avoid gossip at all costs.

'Thank you, gentlemen, for your attendance today. The meeting is now closed.'

All attendees remained silent as they left the pavilion.

Morale was at an all time low and the gossip amongst the villagers is clearly unsubstantiated but hurtful none the less. The ladies who share the green decided that there was no need to call a separate meeting; most of them were married to bowlers and got the news from their husbands.

The outdoor bowling season ran from April to September but the pavilion was in constant use all year socially. Also, repairs and maintenance would be carried out off season.

Graham knew this sad event would remain with the club for many years. Probably even grow in many ways, as all stories.

Chapter 15

All Eyes are now on Jim!

It was clearly a relief for Helen to no longer be a person of interest to the police but, at the same time, impossible to believe that Jim was the only person the police were questioning.

'This is an impossible situation Helen.'

Mike told Helen what Graham had said in the meeting that day and she concurred.

'I know, darling. And, of course there's Kate to consider; she must be at her wits end. All who know Jim will never believe he could hurt Em. They never even quarrelled, according to Em.; Jim is such a gentle person and right now suffering so much.'

Helen added.

'Let's invite Jim, Kate and Simon over for dinner to show our support.'

'Good idea, love, I'll ring and ask right now.'

Kate answered the phone and was delighted to hear Mike's voice.

Kate's response was full of gratitude.

'That's so kind of you both. Everyone seems to be avoiding us all at the moment. I'll just check with the men.'

Less than a second passed.

'Yes, Mike, it's a unanimous thumbs up. They were listening to our conversation.'

They both laughed.

Kate continued.

'Is 7 o'clock okay?'

'We'll be ready for you. Oh! Get a taxi and I'll raid the drinks cabinet.'

Mike chuckled.

'No need for a taxi.' Kate responded. 'I'll drive; I have some news for you.'

Kate hung up just as the penny dropped with Mike.

Promptly, at 7 o'clock the door bell chimed.

As Mike opened the door he joked with his guests.

'So, which one of you is pregnant? I'll take a wild guess, now let me think. Could it be you Kate?'

They all laughed together, something they hadn't done for quite a while.

Jim was a little pensive at times during the evening; but did his best to hide his emotions.

Helen had ready a delicious honey-roast chicken and served it with a selection of vegetables and her secret gravy recipe. Dessert was a homemade apple pie she had waiting in the freezer and topped with custard; every bit was eaten and enjoyed in, almost, silence.

Mike was determined not to talk about the criminal investigation hanging over Jim's head but, of course, it was on everyone's mind.

The subject was becoming more difficult to avoid so around 10.30 Kate stood and said.

'Well, come on boys. A girl in my condition needs her sleep.'

It was a relief as tension was growing. As the visitors left the house there were hugs and thanks for a lovely evening and delicious meal.

As they waved the visitors off and went back indoors, Helen broke down and sobbed in Mike's arms as he spoke.

'How is all this going to end? It can't have been Jim; can it?'

Mike cleared the dining table, loaded the dishwasher and took two brandies into the lounge where Helen was waiting.

They sat for a while, sipping their brandies, until Helen felt calmer and broke the silence.

'You think it was Jim, don't you?'

'Who else could it be, Helen? Not intentional, of course, but a push in temper. I feel so guilty that I made Emily keep that secret of me possibly being her father until the DNA was confirmed. I truly believed that it was impossible to get pregnant after just one liaison; of course I was being hopeful. I just didn't want to spoil our perfect life together, Helen. I am so very sorry.'

Mike put his head in his hands as Helen consoled him.

'Yes darling, you could have managed things differently; but you are not responsible for Emily's death.'

Mike continued.

'The strange thing is that when I showed Jim the letter Joan had written on her deathbed, he was not in the least upset. I explained why we kept the whole thing a secret until the paternity test came back positive and he just smiled. In fact as he smiled he whispered "I knew Em. would never betray me."

If he had killed her before leaving home to come and sit with me, surely he would be upset, devastated even. Then when I gave him the letter explaining everything he was simply relieved and clearly not behaving like a man who had killed his innocent wife.'

Helen put her arm around Mike's shoulder as she spoke.

'It does sound strange. In fact it would be impossible to stay that calm, surely, but who else could it be?'

Jim was up early the next morning. He was sitting at the breakfast table in the kitchen when Simon came in.

'Morning Jim.'

Jim responded.

'Nice of Mike and Helen to invite us over last night, wasn't it?'

'Yes' Simon responded 'unless they were testing us. Until we know for sure what happened the day Emily was killed, everyone is a possible suspect, Jim.'

Jim shook his head.

'Put it this way Jim. With Emily out of the picture no-one would be any the wiser as regards to her paternity.'

'Ah!' Jim responded. 'But he showed me the letter before I discovered Em.'

Simon smirked.

'Okay, you got me there but someone, somewhere will have made a mistake and I will find the guilty party. Trust me Jim.'

When Kate joined the men for breakfast she made an announcement.

'I've decided to pack my job in, guys, and be a kept woman and soon-to-be mother. What do you think?

Simon spoke first.

'That's a great idea, darling.'

Before Jim could make his comment the door bell chimed, it was the police. Jim was arrested for the suspected manslaughter of his wife and taken away in handcuffs.

A bitter sweet morning for the family.

Chapter 16

The Inevitable Happens!

Simon rang Martin before he and Kate followed Jim to the police station. As expected Kate was distraught.

'Why are they taking dad in for questioning yet again? Surely they know everything by now.'

Kate's arm flayed about in the passenger seat next to Simon.

'You need to expect the worst, love. I have a strong feeling this time is to charge Jim.'

'Oh God No!' Kate was becoming hysterical.

When they parked the car Simon spotted Martin walking towards the entrance and called after him. He turned to wait for the couple and they walked in together.

Martin spoke first.

'I think we need to prepare for the worst.'

He looked at Kate as he spoke.

'This is not the end Kate, we'll fight this together. Don't give up.'

They waited in the reception area as Martin and Simon chatted quietly.

'Si, I didn't tell you that I've had a private investigator, a personal friend, digging around. A friendly chat with Jim's neighbours and the like. Just to see if there were any other visitors that day.'

Before they could continue the police officer on reception told Martin he could go through to be with Jim.

That day it was decided that Jim would be charged with manslaughter which carries a custodial sentence. He was to be kept in the police cells overnight and taken to the Magistrates Court in the morning. At the Magistrates Court tomorrow the matters of the case would all be presented to the Bench. The Prosecutor would request that

Jim be remanded in custody due to the seriousness of the crime and, of course, Martin would plead that he is not a flight risk and due to the fact it was a domestic crime that Jim was accused of he is not a risk in the community.

No-one slept that night, including Jim in the police cell.

The morning came and Jim was fed and then taken by an agency vehicle with individual cubicles to the Magistrates Court where he was locked in their cells until his case was called.

An hour of tension and worry later the cell door was open and Martin walked in, he was tense but his purpose was to ensure Jim knew exactly what was to happen that day.

'You are to be seen in courtroom three and you are fourth in line so it may even be that you'll be seen this afternoon. Listen carefully to what I'm telling you, Jim. At this time the most important thing is that you go home tonight rather than remanded in custody. We have to ensure the Magistrates believe that you are not a flight risk or a danger to others. The charge will then be fought in the Crown Court. Do you understand?'

'Yes Martin.'

Jim looked terrified.

Martin continued.

'The prosecutor's job is to get you remanded in custody as it could influence the Crown Court hearing if you are considered dangerous. After giving your plea of not guilty the whole case will be heard today only to establish if you can be released on bail or remanded in custody in prison until the trial.'

If you are spoken to by the Presiding Justice who will sit in the middle on the Bench, today it will be a lady, you must address her as Your Worship or M'am.

When asked for your plea, speak clearly and say 'NOT GUILTY'. Is that clear Jim.'

Martin gave Jim a hug before leaving him alone in his cell once more.

Time passed faster than Jim expected and the cell door opened again. Jim was lead to a staircase that then lead directly to courtroom three; the door was opened at the top of the stairs and the dock was the first door on the right. He was guided in and a security guard sat with Jim in the dock. It proceeded exactly as Martin had said.

The prosecutor on behalf of the Crown, painted a savage, unrecognisable picture of Jim as being the only person in the frame for an attack on a loving, innocent young wife.

The prosecutor added.

'This man then left their home leaving Emily to lay there for hours. What can be more callous?'

He looked at Jim as he spoke.

'And now he lies about the whole thing.'

Then it was Martin's turn. A Kings Council for many years. His job was carried out to perfection.

The Bench retired to make their decision between bail and remand in custody.

When the Bench returned to the Courtroom with their decision the Presiding Justice made an order that both parties; prosecution and defence, share all matters concerning the case before the next hearing, to ensure all evidence is known by all parties. Then she started her pronouncement.

Jim was standing in the dock clutching the handrail and shaking from head to toe.

From start to finish the whole procedure had lasted a couple of hours then the pronouncement was made. Jim was released on conditional bail and walked out of the Courthouse that day to await the Crown Court hearing. He could breathe again, for a while anyway.

Chapter 17

Now the Hard work Begins!

Martin gave Jim two days peace, then, on the third he rang.

'Hi Jim, it's Martin. How are you holding up?'

Jim wanted to respond by saying 'What do you think?' But what was the point of being rude to the one person trying to help.

'Not too bad, Martin. I've been making notes so that I can begin to understand how I got myself into this abominable mess.'

'That's perfect Jim. I know how much the thought of someone believing you could kill the woman you love hurts. This is what we will be depending on when we are in that courtroom fighting for your freedom. We must cast doubt on the Prosecution's case by presenting an emotional aspect of what losing Emily has meant to you. A man who is always thoughtful to others, never known to be angry or lose his temper and a friend to everyone.

'The Jury will be advised by the Presiding Judge to find you innocent if there is any doubt, what so ever, of your guilt. Our job is to install doubt in the minds of that Jury and you will walk free.'

'I am so grateful for your help, Martin. Sometimes I feel as if I'm drowning in an ocean of prejudice. With no-one else to consider for the crime; everyone will believe I must have done it.'

After a moments silence Martin spoke once more.

'When the jury takes a long look at you, as they always do, I pray they will see an innocent man. I will also create options for the jury to consider. They will see that I truly believe in your innocence; so the only thing you have to do in to trust in me.'

'Thank you, Martin, those words of confidence means so much to me.'

'Now, Jim, we have work to do. We need to build our case for your defence. Can you come to my office at 9 a.m. tomorrow? It's important to get our meetings recorded and my secretary to type them up. I can re-read them and build a solid defence.'

'Of course, Martin. See you at 9 a.m. I'll bring all the notes I've made too, they may help.'

Jim wanted to be alone and give Kate and Simon their life back; at least they could begin to plan the birth of their baby without considering him first. The early months of pregnancy can be exhausting with morning sickness that often lasts all day. Being alone would also help Jim focus, getting things straight in his head without interruption. He had told Kate his plan that he wanted time to himself and she didn't try to change his mind.

Jim was also making plans to ensure his business of running the stables would continue in his absence, if the worst happened. He had a great team working for him, many for years, so he selected a manager and put all the details in writing; ensuring a good pay rise for all.

After the meeting with Martin the following day, Jim felt that he was in good hands. He was feeling relieved that there was no more to be done but wait for his day in court.

That evening Kate turned up at her dad's house unexpectedly.

'I really need to speak with you, dad.' Kate had an extremely positive attitude that didn't encourage argument. 'We have a lot to talk about. Don't distract me dad, I have so much to say.'

Jim hugged his daughter like never before. They were both tearful.

'You are my life Katie, my whole world. If it hadn't been for you I would never have met and married Emily. We've both lost so much with all that has happened but you have a future. You have Simon and your new baby to think about.'

'We have to talk, I won't let you go to prison; I can't.'

Jim held her by her small shoulders and gently pushed her away.'

'Go home to your husband, my love. If I need you, I promise that I will ring.'

'But, Dad.'

'Please Katie, do as I say. I have so much to do.'

They hugged once more and, reluctantly, Kate left.

Jim certainly did have a lot to do and it didn't involve his court appearance; his mind was made up.

The following morning he drove into Monmouth town and found a local solicitor that deals with conveyance and other matters that needed sorting out.

He entered the office where a receptionist was waiting. Jim explained his issues were urgent and after showing him to a seat she disappeared upstairs. After a short wait she re-appeared with a young lady who introduced herself and guided Jim to her office upstairs.

As they walked, she explained to Jim.

'I have an hour before my next client.'

As they sat at her desk she spoke.

'Well, sir, what can I do for you?'

Chapter 18

Tying up Loose Ends!

Leaving the solicitors; Jim breathed a sigh of relief. The lady who dealt with him and his requests was efficient and eager to help. Whatever the future held for Jim; Kate would want for nothing. A smile grew on his face as he thought of his grandchild. But, of course, the reality of the situation of him not being around hit him hard. Shaking off the sadness the best he could, Jim decided to call into the bowling green. He was a little nervous. He would soon find out if he had any friends left.

As Jim drove into the car park he noticed there were quite a few cars. His nerves were getting the better of him and he sat for a while. He prayed for compassion.

Leaving the car he walked around the pavilion to the green where a few members were playing a friendly. Jim sat alone and watched in envy; how he loved that game.

Ten minutes passed and he heard a familiar voice call his name as the bowler walked towards him. Allan Spencer was a good friend of many years.

'Jim, it's good to see you. I've wanted to ring you but I thought that you may be angry with me.'

'Why would I be angry with you, Allan? You told the truth and rightly cleared Helen's name.'

Jim stood to greet Allan and the men hugged.

'I just wish I had an alibi, even better I wish I still had my Emily.' He smiled as he spoke to lighten the seriousness of his comment.

'I am so very sorry, Jim. I really am. If it's any consolation, I don't believe for one minute you would hurt anyone, least of all Emily.'

'Thanks Allan, that means a lot.'

With that the game ended, and every bowler walked towards Jim and shook his hand with words of kindness. Tears were shed.

Jim stayed for a while and then decided to go home. That evening he spent his time in deep thought; not about his future but about his past life.

The alarm clock rang at 7 a.m. Jim showered and dressed for the day ahead. Martin wanted to see him.

During the meeting there was a lot of repetition and clarification. Martin remained optimistic but Jim's thoughts were simple; he was the only person in the frame.

If the jury found Jim guilty of manslaughter without intent the judge would decide on the appropriate punishment, but not before Martin would present his mitigation plea.

Martin reminded Jim of the years these judges spend listening to serious cases such as this. They rarely make mistakes.

Jim responded.

'But I am an innocent man.'

It was a long hard day and there would be many more. After several hours Jim left for home, a little down at heart but matters were becoming clearer as to his next big job.

As he settled down to a quiet evening in front of the television the doorbell rang.

He opened the front door and was delighted to see Mike, Dave and a few more bowlers standing there with beer cans in their arms and a smile on their faces. They sat in the lounge and chatted the night away. There were moments of seriousness when loyal support was shown to Jim, but mostly there was laughter which got louder as the beer was consumed.

They stayed until mid-night and left after hugging him. Then silence fell as he sat alone. He decided to finish the last can of beer when his thoughts drifted towards his memories of the fun and happy times he shared with his beloved Em. This reminded Jim of his final task. The letter to Kate. He walked to his study and began typing.

My darling Kate,

These words are just for you. Do not be tempted to share them, not even with Simon. After printing this letter I will delete it from the computer.

As much as I have come to love Simon, I believe the facts as we both know them, could become a burden for him to carry. It is best to sometimes keep secrets well hidden that may hurt others. Allow Simon to love you and your precious unborn just the way he has always loved and known you.

So this decision that I have made will affect you greatly. My choice has been made with thought and understanding, and your future has been utmost on my mind as regards to what I have to say.

You will have been given this letter by my lawyer Martin, within twenty four hours of my demise, with strict instructions that no-one will know anything about it or its existence. As my lawyer he is bound to act in my favour and carry out my last wishes in professional confidence.

Please abide by my request and wishes or my actions will have been in vain. Do this for the love I have for you.

I have given Martin instructions that I want a meeting with him at 9a.m. at my home. My instructions to him are that a key is under the front door mat and he is to enter. He will find me in the lounge in my favourite chair next to the table. On the table will be two sealed letters in a large envelope. The large envelope will be addressed to Martin and inside one letter to him with instructions and this one which will be addressed to you.

Martin's letter is a classical suicide note that will tell the world that I cannot face the future without my Emily and the Crown Court hearing can be cancelled as my demise will inevitably suggest my guilt.

You, my love, know the truth and I have suspected for a while. Firstly when you came to see me and was very distraught begging me to listen gave me understanding that you knew more about Emily's demise. I have taken the responsibility from you as I could not bear to see you in prison, leave your child without a mother and ruin the rest of your life for something I know was an accident. A terrible, terrible accident.

Please accept my decision; it has been made so that you can enjoy a full and happy life. My love for you overrides what you did and I give you my complete forgiveness.

The conformation about the truth was when Martin told me he had used a private investigator and it came to light that you were seen at the entrance of the drive making your way to the house. The time hadn't been recorded and I told Martin it was a visit to see me and Em. two hours before I left the house to sit with Mike for Helen to clean the pavilion. I also told him that we all had coffee and you left with a book you were borrowing from Emily.

I had already sensed you were hiding something from me and at times was eager to share. I know you so well, my darling Katie. I knew you were on the verge of spilling the beans. You have shown total support for me, telling all and sundry I was innocent and you knew I didn't kill Em. You must have been so scared but it's over now.

BURN THIS LETTER SWEETHEART!!!

I love you Katie xxx

The end

A few extras in the form of:-

'LETTERS'

&

'POEMS'

This is the story of a young Welsh girl who is 'in service' to a wealthy English family living in London. This scenario was common years ago and life-changing for many but most did their time and returned to the Welsh valleys. Whether speaking or writing the accent always seems to come through; also Ceinwen's naivety as the tale unfolds.

A Letter Home   by   Lynne Rees-Tippett

305 Temple Gardens

Paddington

London W1

27th May 1928

Dear Mam and Dad,

I hope you are well Mam, and not working too hard. It has been nine months since I came down here to London and I am sorry to say I don't like it one bit. Wyn said not to tell you but I can't help how I feel, I miss you and Dad and last night I cried myself to sleep. Don't worry Mam, I'll get used to it.

Wyn and me are good friends and now that we share a room I am feeling a bit better. Annie is nice too. We have got to get up at 5 o'clock in the morning to set the grates; I bet you are managing without fire due to it getting a bit warmer, that will save you a few bob now that Dad's not working.

I have put a shilling in with this letter to help out a bit. Tell dad to have a penny or two for baccy and you get tuppence for some nice sweets for yourself. I wish I could send more, I know times are hard.

You should see the house Mam, it is so big I keep getting lost. I think Mr and Mrs Harcombe must be high up to have so many people working for them.

Me and Wyn went out to look in the shops for a bit yesterday, you'd never believe the price of cloth down here Mam, silk and everything they got. When I've got money I will buy some cloth for you to sew up, you can make a nice dress for chapel.

Mrs Harcombe gave me one of her old dresses yesterday, navy blue with cream lace around the neck. I'll keep it for best. She said my best one was looking tight, she's good like that Mam, very kind to us all.

I am walking out with a gentleman Mam he's high up in service and Mr Harcombe's driver. Joseph is his name, a bit posh but he said he likes me a lot.

You should see the parlour Mam, thick carpet and the curtains are so heavy it takes three of us to take them down for cleaning. And the china, well it's all the same, they have cups and saucers with the same pattern on as the plates, you'd love it.

I heard Mr Harcombe talking to one of his posh friends yesterday when I was bringing their tea. He said that Churchill was good to sort out those miners in Wales 'cause they were out of control. Well I nearly told him Mam, those miners have given their lives for our pits and people shouldn't talk about them like that. Ten years on and they are still talking about the Tonypandy Riots. Well I am proud of what they done Mam and I very nearly told 'um too but I was afraid to speak out. It do make me mad though.

Have our Blod had the baby yet Mam she must be about due? I hope it's a boy she said she would call him after our Dad.

I can hardly see by this candle. Wyn have put hers out and she's fast asleep.

Joseph mended my shoes for me last week, they were letting the wet in. Wyn and Annie have known Joseph for a bit now and said they have never known him to take a fancy to a parlour maid before, I must be special they said.

I have got two rasberry ruffles left from the bag that Joseph bought me Saturday, I have one every night before I go to sleep.

When is our Dai getting wed to that girl he's been courting? They can live with her mother and give our Stan and Will more room, they are too big to be three in a bed now.

Did I tell you Mam, Annie is Welsh, she is from Treochi, she said you will know her Mam cause she is from Pandy. Her Dad worked in the Camb. before they moved, ask Dad if he knows him, his name is Will Jones. Annie said her Dad was in the big fall in Camb. that killed Mrs Davies the milks boy.

You should give our Blod a dose of caster oil Mam that will move the baby.

I have been bad lately, must be something I have eaten, I was sick this morning and Wyn gave me some peppermint. Didn't work though.

Joseph said he likes a girl to carry a bit of weight it means there is more to cwtch, he's a boy aye Mam. He's knows about life 'cause he was in the war, tall too, I am only up to his shoulder.

We have lots to do tomorrow Mr Harcombe is having people to dinner, Joseph said they are royalty but I think he is teasing me, he is always teasing me.

I got to put my pen down a minute Mam my skirt is killing me.

Right o, I got my nighty on now, my skirt has made a red mark around my waist, I will have to move the button.

Joe have been saving to take me out on our next day off together. A place called Drury Lane, have you heard of it Mam? A famous man called Ivor Novello has written a show called Glamorous Nights. Joe said he is Welsh so I should enjoy it.

Well Mam I think I'll close now, I am so tired. The last few weeks I get tired so quick.

Give Phyllis a kiss from me and tell her to work hard in school.

Your ever loving daughter

Ceinwen

....

Did you guess why Ceinwen's skirt was getting tight ???

The following two poems are relevant to this letter and an important part of the history of the Rhondda valley and Tonypandy in particular............................

Cambrian Colliery

I was born into the fifties, rationing was at an end;

Things were getting better, a little more to spend.

Life was full of promise, a good living in the mines;

By the time we reached the sixties standards improved with time.

I was on an errand for my Nan, when came that dreadful sound,

Air piercing sirens saying "Disaster underground".

I stood frozen on the pavement as the engines thundered past;

Cambrian Colliery, Clydach Vale; many lost in the blast.

I remember the people running, all racing to the head,

So many gathered silently, there was nothing to be said.

Bodies brought up one by one, someone's husband, father, son.

Women stood together, silent tears watched rescue done.

So many lives affected by that godforsaken day.

Proud, hardworking, loyal men were cruelly snatched away.

Now in my sixties I walk those hills and take a break to sit.

I think about that teenage day and the disaster in our pit.

17th May 1965. 31 Miners Lost in the P26 Gas Explosion

The Tonypandy Riots

I didn't know the hardship endured for you and me,

I didn't understand the reasons and the fight to make me free.

The gallantry of the miners who accepted poverty

As part of their desperate struggle and betterment for me.

I thank you, men of Rhondda, for the fight you strongly lead.

I thank you for proud actions and words you left unsaid.

The fight through brave endurance, too many left unfed;

The Tonypandy miners, your memory never dead.

One hundred years have come and gone, but we remember all;

The conflicts caused by lockouts, hungry colliers standing tall.

The striking and the pickets 'til the army had their call;

Did Churchill send the Hussars to cause the miners fall?

Cwmardy tells the story, of the riots by Jones was penned,

Lewis was just a valley boy when called as a miner, to defend.

When the Combine and its members refused their will to bend,

But stood so strong and fought together until their winning end.

The mountains of our valley have turned from grey to green,

As the mines have closed one by one n'er more to be seen.

No more slag upon our hills or coal raised from the seams;

The buckets on the hillside no longer part of the team.

One miner lost in battle; we can't celebrate the fight;

But we can in their achievement and the glory of their might.

We have great men of Rhondda, their memory we hold tight,

A pride unique to our valley, an everlasting light.

....

1st August 1910 – Lockout at Ely pit, Penygraig, Rhondda.

By 7th November 1910 – All striking pits were picketed except for one.

Thousands of miners gathered and marched down through the Rhondda.

The one pit still working was in Llwynypia it housed a generator and pumping station that kept the mine from flooding. Police from Swansea, Bristol and Cardiff were drafted in to guard this pit.

7th & 8th November 1910 the famous Tonypandy Riots took place.

500 colliers were injured, Samuel Rhys died from injuries caused by a policeman's baton.

The whole episode lasted one year then the miners returned to work with a small pay increase.

A letter written by a young man just out of Eton and on a gap year in Brazil.

Somewhere in the jungle
North of Manaus
Amazonia/Manaus
Brazil.

1ˢᵗ April 2014.

My Dearest Mother,

I am please to say that I have a window in my busy life to write and tell you of my adventures in the magnificent Rain Forests of Brazil. I must say Mother; I was not expecting such demands to be made on both my time and abilities. It seems that the local people work quite hard with little reward and are unbelievably happy with their lot, quite amazing.

I know I promised to write every week but you must understand that life here is not like Henley on Thames. The River Amazon is unbelievably different to the Thames in every way possible. We get up early in the morning having slept in hammocks swinging from the walls of our cabin. If we place our mosquito nets in the advised manner we may get away without being eaten alive, as yet I have not achieved this. Fortunately for me, one of the boys has a tube of something called DEAT which he plasters on my lumps and bumps for me.

On occasion I realise this working gap year to enhance my Eton education and the whole idea of living the local life in Brazil is not completely what I anticipated. I must admit I have looked for better accommodation; but there just isn't anything. Perhaps we should have chosen somewhere less exotic but the pictures did look so inviting.

Having taken some advice and we've been travelling with qualified guides. It seems that some villages are hostile and are best avoided. One day seems to melt into another until, as in this instance, five whole months have past by and I find myself trying to catch up with my correspondence and duties as a good son.

I really must say Mother, I was quite upset and disappointed that you contacted the Embassy telling them I was missing, having not heard from me for a while. Sending out a search party didn't help matters only alienated them and caused a great deal of embarrassment to my friends and me. They caught up with us in Manaus where it was suggested that I go home and stay there until I'd grown up enough to travel. Upon which they checked my visa and glared at me with a look of disbelief when they saw my age. I ventured a comment "Yes I am twenty two years of age Sir, but my mother worries".

They allowed Alex to assume responsibility for me, as he is the eldest in our group, and with apologies from us all they allowed us to go on with our travels.

So much has happened I just don't know where to begin. Well, Christmas was of little importance, as you can imagine, but George, Alex, Harry and I had lunch together in a street café in Manaus overlooking the river. We celebrated the festive occasion by drinking some local brew served in huge glass barrels on each table with a tap at the base to fill our glasses from. The meal wasn't very festive but we enjoyed fried chicken and fried chunks of sweet potato; I don't recall the name of the ale but its brewed locally and they say it helps to relieve tension; the locals are all extremely relaxed. Everyone seems to smoke too, in cafes and shops, there's no restriction. The cigarettes smell a little strange and the air has a sweet scent. Oh yes! I've overcome my terror of rats. When drinking at a street bar of an evening; at any one time you can count over fifty rats scurrying around. The first time I saw the rats I was in a state of paralysed shock until the tail of one stroked my ankle at which point I ran for the nearest chair. But I'm fine with them now.

As it was the dry season in January we set off on a trek further into the jungle. We spent many hours walking through the rainforest and finding villages normally cut off by the swollen river. One of our best adventures was when we walked into a clearing to find ten houses in a circle. There were naked children playing in the middle, women preparing food and dogs lazing in the heat of the sun. I am embarrassed to say the lavatorial facilities were extremely basic and they had no running water. However, to my great disbelief they had Sky television run by generators. In my opinion they have their priorities perfectly arranged.

On one of our treks we found a very friendly village and were invited to stay for the night. We shared their food, I decided not to ask what it was, and we partook of their herbal drink which tasted a little suspicious but that was the least of our worries. The Coca plant is growing wild and I enjoyed a few spliffs, purely medicinal of course

Mother, it helps me to cope with the heat. Three days later I woke up, and started the trek back with a few gifts from the Chief, just in case I need the medicine again. He seemed to like me but I really can't think why. My memories are confused; I get flash backs of me dancing naked around the fire but that is not like me at all so I think they must just be vivid dreams caused by the coca.

We've made good friends, some young men who are interested in finding out more about England. I gave them your address and told them you'd love to have them stay. Some speak good English and I've surprised myself by actually picking up a few phrases of Portuguese and the local dialect too. The girls are especially interesting but I'm not sure you'd like them Mother, they are quite scantily clad, some even less.

Our guides, Miguel and Juan, took the four of us on a night time Safari to see the Caiman Alligators and the Anacondas; as they sleep all day. The canoe was a little small for us all and we had a few scares, especially when George fell over board trying to take a photo of Miguel holding a three foot Caymen by his tail. He made such a dreadful fuss, cried like a baby. I took a video of it all but stopped when I realised the piranha were trying to eat his toes and helped pull him out. I'm glad to say he's all in tact but I'm keeping the video as security, you never know when a favour is needed and I have his trainers as well, no toes in them of course.

The rainy season has begun and our cabins are floating on logs anchored to the river bed. The river rises by eighteen foot at this time of year. Our only means of transport is our little boat, but all is good. The petrol stations are floating in the middle of the river, it looks quite extraordinary.

Before I conclude, I have some rather special news for you. I realise that this may come as a shock to you and Father but I don't think I will be home anytime soon. It appears that the night I spent in that village with the nice Chief, I seem to have had more fun than I actually remember. She is the chief's second daughter, Marla, and it seems I was naked after all. I'll let you know if it's a boy or girl and maybe you could come and visit. Bring Father he'd like the ladies fashions.

Your ever loving son - Giles

P.S. You've probably noticed the date Mother, but this is no joke.

I have personally had some experience of this part of the world but my husband and I didn't venture too far from the Amazon river, and there was certainly no drug-taking!

My last offering is two of my short poems about Rotary and Inner Wheel.

Firstly a little about Inner Wheel.

Inner wheel began as a result of Rotary. Margarette Peggy Golding, wife of a Rotarian was a Welsh born nurse and business woman who started life in Blaenau Ffestiniog 20th November 1881, she passed away at the age of 59 but in her life she made her name as founder of Inner Wheel. Both Rotary and Inner Wheel have clubs and members all over the world and work hard to ensure those who are in need get the support and help they deserve. Both associations welcome new members at all times.

The Family of Rotary

When dawn arrives and day begins I often wonder why
God chooses some to have so much that others are denied.

We measure life with owning things, things that money buys.

When what we should be counting is the happiness in our lives.

The poverty and hardship that so many have to bear

Sickness, war, starvation; children alone – without care.

Rotary, a universal force stands strong against all odds

Working for the betterment of life throughout the world.

Rotarian clubs breed fellowship; friendship and loyalty

Members standing up for right, and doing so happily.

Caring for communities both at home and far away

Working in relentless harmony, improving day by day.

The Adventures of Getting Old

It seems like only yesterday that I was twenty one,

No aching joints to stop me having all that fun.

Energy abounding, so necessary to the young,

Planning a happy future with many years to come.

They say the body falters with encroaching middle age,

It must have been around the time I started wearing beige.

From that point on, I must admit, things do go down that hill;

The kids have gone, you have it made, and then come all those pills.

They become the main ingredient in conversation with your friends;

Blood pressure, cholesterol and backache, joints that refuse to bend.

Don't ever underestimate the power of getting on,

You find so many like you, you enjoy the aging bond.

The real comedy of aging is when the mem'ry goes,

Guess where you've parked the car at Tesco's; it keeps you on your
toes.

Lists become important, then finding them again,

And reciting the alphabet silently, great for remembering names.

The one thing I've found that helps me, is the fact that we're all the same;

Learning to laugh at ourselves, 'cause there's no-one else to blame.

In fact it's quite refreshing, aging as we do;

With a knowing smile to youngsters, heading that way too.

Perhaps it's one of the reasons that Inner Wheel succeeds,

The wisdom of common experience; helping those in need.

Enjoying the company of ladies who have passed the aging test

Standing together proudly; amongst the very best.

This is definitely the end !!!

Printed in Great Britain
by Amazon